GRITTY SOUTHERN *Christmas* ANTHOLOGY

First Edition

Gritty South
GrittySouth.com
Printed in the United States

This work is based on the authors' personal perspective and imagination.

Editor and Interior Designer– Rachel Davis
Publisher – Angela Broyles

Library of Congress Control Number: 2021945299

Perfect Bind book ISBN: 9781949711899
eBook ISBN: 9781949711882

Table of Contents

Racially Content at Christmastime

Remind them
Jesus Black.
Despite the pictures Granny
has hung on the wall,
despite the glowing good ole boy
on her pile of church fans,
Jesus was a brother.
A bruh, not a bro.
Hair of wool, you tell them.

Buy a new nativity set.
Mary with her press and curl,
Joseph with a fade,
baby Jesus fresh out the womb
and curly.

Go to a roadside Christmas shop.
Buy a pale, smiling Santa.
Let your daughters wonder
how he turned brown overnight—
how Santa's face became just like their own,
brown and buttery, a Yuletide miracle.

When you're trimming your plastic tree—
the one you've had since the 80's,
put on "Rudolph" bopped by the Temptations,
"Deck the Halls" by Smokey,
Donny Hathaway's "This Christmas,"

and Gladys Knight's deep, brown voice crooning "Jingle
Bells."
Fill the treeskirt
with tightly-wrapped gifts.
Anticipate
your daughters' unbreakable smiles

when they rip off the paper
to reveal an army

of Black Barbies
and brown baby dolls.

Ashley Jones

Hooves and Hope

C. R. Fulton

I don't have any parents, none that want me anyway. That's why I've been condemned to spending my two-week Christmas break in the boondocks of Kentucky. *Sullen.* That's how my caseworker describes me. I prove it as we turn into a long gravel drive lined with deep potholes. The car lurches, upsetting soda all over my lap.

"What a beautiful farm," she says, gripping the wheel. She had been nervous on the flight. She'd wanted to talk to cover it up. Eventually I'd held up a sheet of paper with "Lacey Mullins doesn't care" written on it. That had silenced her, but it hadn't changed this trip or reversed our direction. I'm still here, exactly where I don't want to be.

I open my phone. "Zero bars." The words come out like a curse.

The driveway turns left and a white house with huge black barns behind it comes into view. A big cow stares at me through the fence wearing a lump of hay on its head. I almost laugh, but that's too dangerous, like doing a drug I can't get more of.

I clutch my phone as I step out of the car, the woman on the porch must be my aunt Rose. She looks nothing like my mother. Her salt-and-pepper hair is up in a messy bun but it's her bright brown eyes that catch me. They're the same color as mine. What's she got to look so happy about?

"Hello, Lacey. Welcome to the bluegrass." I frown at her as a cat with a white tip on its tail rubs against my legs.

"Excuse me," I mutter to it as I trudge through the wet grass to the porch.

The scent of animals makes me cringe…it's something you don't deal with in Buffalo, New York. Course, it's thirty degrees colder there too.

"Come on, I'll show you to your room," Rose says. The house is simple and clean. A huge wooden Nativity takes up one corner of the living room.

"You're missing something," I say, looking at the empty manger surrounded by the other exquisite figures.

"Jesus didn't arrive till Christmas morning. It's not time for him to be there yet," she says with a twinkle in her gaze.

I scowl at the manger. There's a pitiful wisp of straw in the bottom of it. "Could you spare the straw?"

Rose looks at me with one side of her mouth pulled back. What do I care if I upset her? I didn't want to come here anyway.

"I have a feeling there will be plenty by the twenty-fifth." I snort through my nose at her reply. "Your room's upstairs, come on."

She leaves me to settle in. I finger the quilt that's an explosion of color, definitely not my style, then look out the window. There are more cows than I'd ever seen at once, and a flock of geese waddle through the yard. I catch my breath. Behind the barns, horses graze. I watch them until a commotion downstairs draws me in.

I descend the stairs to see two teenagers hugging Rose. I cross my arms against the sight. It's not like I need that sort of thing.

"Grammy, did Moonlight have her foal yet?" a girl about my age asks.

"Nope. She's hanging on to him for now." Rose looks up to find me glaring at them. "This is Lacey, your cousin."

The younger boy says, "Hello." I nod, but clamp my jaw shut. He looks up at Rose in question and she points down the hallway. "Would you get the paints?" They disappear down the hall, chattering happily to each other. Don't they have perfect little lives?

"Alana and Jaden are my grandchildren; we paint every Tuesday. You will treat them with respect while you are here." The front door opens and a gray-haired man steps in.

"You must be Lacey. Nice to meet you. I'm Jeff."

I cringe inside. Men have always taken from me, one way or the other. I struggle to maintain my brash attitude and say nothing. Rose and Jeff exchange glances. I bet they regret having me here. Alana and Jaden rush toward Jeff, their arms loaded with acrylic paints. He hugs them tight, all smiles and love.

It's as foreign to me as the German class I usually skip at school. "I've got to run to town for parts," he says, and I follow Rose to the dining room. She slides a blank canvas in front of me.

"What will go good with red and green?" Alana asks.

"What about white and gold?" Rose says.

Soon there are colors everywhere, except on my canvas. Rose pushes a jar of brushes in my direction. I've never painted before.

"Fine." I grumble, grabbing the black and red paints. The wet colors are mesmerizing as I push them across the canvas, absorbed by the way they mix.

It doesn't look like anything, just bursts of color, but it's strangely satisfying and I forget to scowl.

"Jaden, did you water the horses last time you were here?" He nods at Rose's question. "Thank you. Why don't you put some straw in the manger?"

His eyes brighten as he grins. I watch him rip a big handful from a bag of straw that I hadn't noticed before. He puts it reverently in the bottom of the manger. I look up to find Rose watching me. "That's why there wasn't much straw on the manger to begin with. Every kind act gains you the right to help prepare the manger for baby Jesus. One handful at a time. We better have it full by Christmas when he arrives."

Six days later

I shove my fingers under the rough twine on the heavy hay bale. I heave it up, forcing it higher with one knee.

"You've gotten better at that," Rose says as she stacks the bale in the truck.

"Didn't have much choice."

"True." She says with a smile. "Five more should do."

Actually, I sort of enjoy the hard work and the burn in my muscles. It feels good. I ride on the bales as she drives into the horse pasture.

The herd swirls around us, snatching hay off the truck. Three little foals prance around their mothers. They are the cutest things on the planet.

"You think Moonlight will have her baby today?"

Rose scowls at a black mare whose stomach is stretched tight. "At this point, I'm done guessing. She's three weeks late and that baby's only getting bigger. Could spell trouble for her." The horse nips at her side and Rose says, "I'll put her in the foaling stall today, just in case." We finish feeding in silence. I rub Moonlight's velvety nose and she snorts, making me jump.

"Come on Lacey, it's time for lunch. Jeff should be back from the feed store soon." The cat with a white-tipped tail curls around my legs and I stroke her arched back. I've discovered that I like animals more than I do most people. Except for the geese. The seven of them terrify me.

"Bo, don't chase the cows," Rose scolds at the big white dog that's usually on the porch. It's like living in a zoo.

We ride up to the house and Rose turns to me. "Did we turn the water off?" I roll my eyes, trying to remember. "Could you go check? It'll make a muddy mess if it overflows."

"If you insist." I sigh.

Trudging back down to the barn, I think about the days that have passed since I texted friends back home. I've groused plenty about it and I know I've been pushing Rose to the end of her patience. The gate creaks as I push through and see the cattle's water is off. My stomach growls as I round the barn. A loud honk makes me press back against the barn wall. *They're right there.* I can see their huge orange feet under the fence. My heart is in my stomach as I watch them waddle my direction. Terror keeps me frozen as the rough barn wood bites into my back.

The lead goose rounds the corner, its long head drops low as it hisses at me. The other six rush forward and the whole flock spread out their wings, charging toward me. I scream for all I'm worth and barely touch the wooden fence as I vault over it.

I've caught my breath by the time I reach the house and I walk in like nothing's happened.

"It was off anyway. What a bunch of wasted effort." I plunk at the table, staring at the Nativity. The manger is almost full of straw.

"Why don't you have a Christmas tree?" The question comes out as a demand.

Rose sets a platter full of sandwiches on the table. "When I finally finished with the Nativity, the tree seemed meaningless compared to it. After all, Christmas is about Jesus and I like to keep it that way."

"You carved the Nativity?"

She nods, "Took me a few years to finish all the figures, but I learned a lot about each one. How seriously Joseph took his responsibility for God's son. Can you imagine how it must've burdened him to find nowhere but a barn for Jesus to be born in?"

I stare at the intricate figures that look so lifelike. The front door opens and Jeff steps in. Rose hugs him and gives him a kiss. My face flames red.

"How you doing, Lacey?" Jeff asks. I try to swallow down my long-held dislike of men. He'd done nothing to deserve it, but I only manage a shrug.

Jeff's face goes pale as he looks past me out the window. In an instant I know what it is. I'd forgotten to shut the cow gate when I ran from the geese. I turn to find the herd of cattle flowing like a wild river into the wide open.

Rose drops the bowl of chips. She and Jeff bolt for the door. I cover my mouth and blink back tears as I run after them. They will hate me now, surely.

Jeff floors his truck full of feed, fishtailing and ripping up mud. The lead cow sees him shouting out his cattle call and veers toward him wanting feed.

Rose pulls the gate further open as Jeff leads the parade back through. Five refuse to go back in for the grain that he dumps. Instead they buck and run throwing clumps of mud high. Rose puts a hand over her heart as Jeff walks out with the feed bucket. They try to round up the remaining cows.

"Lacey, stand there and wave your arms if they split toward you," Rose shouts.

My knees are trembling as I step forward. This is my fault. How stupid am I? It occurs to me that one of the cows is bigger than the others, with heavy shoulders and a wide head. The bull. Jeff hisses at the herd and they shift toward the gate. The bull's eyes roll white, and time slows down as he turns toward me. I shout with my hands in the air, but he lowers his head and picks up speed. One more stride and he'll smash me. My legs refuse to run, frozen in place.

Jeff tackles me from the side, the bull twisting in midstride, and Jeff bellows in pain as he covers me. Time snaps back to normal and I scramble on hands and knees for the fence. Rose is screaming as the bull rams Jeff again. A streak of white leaps over Jeff's inert form. Bo. His huge mouth clamps on the bull's nose and they spin away from Jeff's still form. Rose is there as Jeff groans, "I'm all right."

"You are going to the hospital."

"No," he sits up, grimacing. "He only got my leg. I'll be fine."

"I'm getting the car."

"Lacey, you okay?" I creep forward at his question. Bo's deep bark makes me jump as he surges at the bull on the far end of the yard.

"I'm… I'm fine."

Jeff takes my hand, "He was coming for you, wasn't he?" I nod as the car pulls up to us.

Jeff stifles a groan while Rose helps him into the car. "Go on inside, I'll call you on the house phone from the hospital."

An icy wind bites my face as they pull out. I hadn't even said thank you to him. I run for the empty house and tears start to flow. Standing in front of the Nativity I replay how Jeff had taken my place. Taken the brutal punishment that should've been mine. It was my fault, the whole thing. Maybe I'd been wrong to hate all men for what my father had done.

I touch Mary's wooden face, *What if I'd been just as wrong about the son she bore?* The phone rings, making me jump. How long have I stood here?

"He's got a fractured femur, but it sure could've been a lot worse. I'll be back in two hours. Are you okay?"

"Yeah. Tell him thank you. I'm so sorry, Rose."

"I'll tell him. He'll be just fine. It was an accident, Lacey. Listen, there's a big bone on top of the fridge. I was saving it for Christmas, but give it to Bo now, will you? He's a good boy."

I hang up the phone and use two hands to lug the bone to the front porch. Bo jumps for it and I sit next to him as he gnaws it, his tail thumping happily. Snowflakes start to float down as I warm my fingers in his fur.

The cattle that are still loose huddle in front of the gate. They want to go in. I guess there's no feed for them out here. I grit my teeth. If I sneak along the inside of the fence, maybe I can open the gate.

By the time I'm near the gate latch, my fingers are trembling. The bull pushes forward as I swing the gate open. I keep it between us for protection and they all run straight in towards the hay bales. Locking the gate, I let out a relieved breath. I race up to the house to burn up the extra adrenaline.

By the time Rose pulls in, I've cleaned up the chips she'd dropped and put away the sandwiches.

"Did you get the cows back in?" she asks. I nod, but I can't get my eyes to meet hers. "And you cleaned up in here?" She waits until I look at her. "Lacey?" I meet her eyes. "He's going to be just fine." I fiddle with the hem of my shirt. "Why don't you get a handful of straw for the manger?"

My mouth falls open. "Really?"

She smiles and draws me into a hug. "Really."

I pull off the biggest handful I can, then spread it carefully in the manger. It has to be just right for when baby Jesus arrives.

"We'd better go check on Moonlight before it gets dark," Rose says.

I gasp as I look out the window, everything is white. "How much snow are we going to get?"

Rose laughs, "After the day we've had, it could be four feet. Let's bundle up."

Moonlight paces the sawdust in her stall and sweats. "Finally," Rose says. "Run for hot water from the house, will you?" By the time Rose has everything she wants, the mare is laying on her side, straining. I grip the stall bars. Transfixed.

"I don't like the looks of this. Don't do this without Jeff here, Moonlight."

"What's wrong?" I question, heart in my throat.

"She's not making any progress. We'll give her another hour, but something's not right." I keep my nose pressed to the bars as the horse gets up and down, groaning. I check the clock, but the minutes creep by.

"Okay, that's it. Scrub your hands, she needs our help." Rose pours iodine on our hands and arms and ties Moonlight in the corner.

She examines her and lets out a sharp breath. "Both front legs are folded back. He can't be born that way. We'll have to reposition him."

"We?"

"My hands aren't strong enough to grip like they used to. Nobody else can come in this weather. I need you, Lacey."

I nod, numb. "Okay."

Rose struggles for a long time until finally she has one front hoof visible. "Okay, take this hoof and hang onto it. It's slippery and it won't be an easy job. Getting that one straightened out was the easy one, the next will be far more difficult."

"What if we can't do it?"

"We'd lose them both. With even one leg folded back there's no way this foal can be born, both front legs have to be straight in order to fit."

I hesitate before grasping the wet little hoof. It's warm, and softer than I'd expected it to be.

"Hold on for all your worth and don't let go." She goes to work on the second leg, and I grit my teeth as the hoof tries to disappear.

"Come on," Rose groans. "There, okay, hang on now. I've got hold of it, but I'll have to push this shoulder back in order to unfold the leg. We've got to work quick here, he's been stuck a while."

I adjust my grip, focusing on the tiny life in my hands. "Okay, go!" Rose and I grunt and growl as she works. Moonlight steps to the side. "Stay with her, Lacey. We're almost there." The other hoof appears. Rose sags in relief.

"Okay, you can let go. I'll unclip her. She should be able to do the rest." Moonlight lays down and in two big pushes a coal black foal slides into the world. Tears stream down my face as the foal's little head comes up off the floor.

Rose throws one arm around my shoulder, "Would of lost them both if you hadn't been here. That was a two-person job. Looks like a filly. What should we name her?"

"Luna," I answer without hesitation.

"I like it," Rose says. I stay with Luna as she wobbles to her feet for the first time. I'm glued by her side while she nurses from her mama, until I'm deeply in love with the coal black filly... Rose forces me inside around one in the morning. I dream of nothing but Luna.

The next morning I'm up early, rushing down to the barn. Rose finds me with Luna's head on my lap.

"They've got the roads clear. I'm going to bring Jeff home. I suppose you want to stay here?" I smile and nod as Luna pushes her tiny muzzle into my elbow. I cradle the soft feeling of happiness that bubbles up from deep inside. Being with Luna is like living for the first time.

Rose interrupts my thoughts, "Come on up for lunch." I look up in surprise, it seemed like five minutes had passed instead of three hours. "Was the ride hard on Jeff?"

"Oh, he's a tough, old farmer, it's not the first time he's broken a bone. He's grumpy about sitting on the couch already though."

We eat lunch in the living room with Jeff. Deep in my heart, I tuck away the knowledge that he'd thought I was worth saving. Rose and I take the dishes into the kitchen.

"Lacey, there's something I need to talk to you about. I spoke with your caseworker, and it's possible, just possible mind you, that you could live here. Permanently. We'd have a lot of legal battles to fight. And the last thing I'd want to be doing is fighting with you at the same time. I would need to know that you want to be here. That you want a shot at a clean slate and a new life." She rubs her hands together nervously. "If that's what you want, and if you work hard and learn a lot, when Luna turns two, you'll be the first person to ride her. Jeff and I, we want to love you day by day, the way you deserve. I know there will be big issues to work through but..." she trails off

Sullen. I look inside, but the word doesn't describe me anymore. My hands, they can still feel Luna's tiny little hoof and the rough, pokey straw that I'd settled into the manger. The things I've experienced here had affected me on the inside more than the outside. I didn't know it was possible to be so full.

"Are you sure Jeff wants me here?" I can barely hold her gaze. How could he, after what I'd done?

"Against my better judgment!" He shouts from the other room. I roll my eyes at his playful tone.

“I…I'd like to stay.” Rose pulls me into a hug that I don't resist.

“Rose, can I put baby Jesus in the manger Christmas morning?” I look at it as she hugs me. It's brimming with soft, bright straw to welcome Him.

“Sure thing. I told you there would be enough when the time came.”

Stille Nacht

Pete Black

"Peace on earth will come to stay, when we live Christmas every day."
Helen Steiner Rice

December 24, 1914 – Ploegsteert Wood, Belgium: Charles Brewer, a nineteen-year-old British lieutenant with the Bedfordshire Regiment, shivered in the muddy trench. Suddenly, he heard someone singing and the song pierced the silence of the clear, cold, moonlit night. Although the words were not familiar to the soldier, the tune certainly was *Silent Night.*

Brewer slowly raised his head above the wet sandbags. Less than eighty yards away, he saw an amazing sight. It was a Christmas tree shining above the wall of the German trench. Gazing through the maze of barbed wire and down the line of trenches, Brewer saw a whole string of Christmas trees lit with candles. When the German soldier finished singing *Stille Nacht,* the British soldiers applauded. Then they sang the English version of the carol.

World War I began June 28, 1914, with the assassination of Archduke Franz Ferdinand of Austria. After the murder, Austria threatened war on Serbia. Within a week, Germany declared war on Russia and France. On August 4, following Germany's attack on France and Belgium, England declared war on Germany.

The main theater of fighting in WWI was along the Western front—a 500-mile line that snaked north from southern Germany through France and Belgium ending at the North Sea. In a matter of months, the fighting had bogged down to trench warfare with soldiers camped in trenches, sometimes only fifty yards apart, all along the front.

Pope Benedict XV, who took office in September 1914, called for a Christmas truce but military leaders rejected his proclamation. Then German, French, and British senior officers issued orders that any soldier caught fraternizing with the enemy would be court martialed.

No one is sure where it began or how it spread, but all along the Western Front soldiers decided to stage their own spontaneous Christmas truce. Almost always, it was the Germans who started the truce.

The truce allowed the soldiers an opportunity to bury the dead, many of whom had been lying frozen in "no man's land" for weeks. It was the first order of business and enemies labored side by side to complete the somber task.

Most often the truce began with Christmas carols. At Flanders in northern Belgium, German soldiers began the cease-fire by holding up a sign that read: "We no shoot, if you no shoot." In France, German soldiers came out of the trenches shouting "Merry Christmas!" Men played an improvised game of soccer in the afternoon using a can for the ball; the game ended in a tie. In one location, there was a pig roast. All along the front, soldiers exchanged gifts of cigarettes, food, beer, liquor, hats, and buttons.

When dawn broke on Christmas morning in Ploegsteert Wood, the German soldiers tentatively climbed out of their trench and walked across "no man's land" to greet Charlie Brewer and his fellow soldiers, men they had been trying to kill only hours before. The soldiers chatted and laughed like they were old friends.

At sunset on Christmas Day, the soldiers retreated to their trenches and at midnight, the fighting resumed. In Houplines, in northern France, Charles Stockwell, a British captain, fired three shots in the air and raised a sign that read, "Merry Christmas." His German counterpart raised a sign that said, "Thank you." The two men saluted each other. The Germans fired two shots in the air and the war was on again.

The guns of World War I would not be silent until the signing of the armistice on November 11, 1918. Though the death toll was never accurately known, it is estimated that more than ten million men died along the Western Front.

The world was different that Christmas Day 1914. Temporarily transformed by the magic of Christmas that touched the hearts of soldiers. Ever so briefly it reminded them what was really important. They put down their weapons, stepped out of their trenches, and for a few precious hours He was in their hearts. Emmanuel—God with us. On an ugly battlefield, God was there.

REFERENCES

Bajekal, Naina. "Silent Night: The Story of the World War I Christmas Truce of 1914." Time Magazine. December 24, 2014.

Dash, Mike. "The Story of the World War I Christmas Truce." Smithsonian Magazine. December 23, 2011. https://www.smithsonianmag.com/history/the-story-of-the-wwi-christmas-truce-11972213/.

Klein, Christopher. "World War I's Christmas Truce." History.com. Updated October 15, 2018. https://www.history.com/news/world-war-is-christmas-truce-100-years-ago.

Weintraub, Stanley. Silent Night: The Story of the World War I Christmas Truce. (New York City: Plume Publishing, 2002).

The Gift

Gayle Young

Brett and Kelli, ages three and four, had gone with their father to his parents' home for Christmas Eve. It was my fault. I'd had the explosion that ended my marriage, and now I had to share my children. I loved my husband and his family and at that minute my greatest desire was to go to them, ask their forgiveness, and stay for dinner and presents. But something inside me wouldn't let me. Some insidious memory or thought so deep I could neither find it nor articulate it, a yearning for something I couldn't understand, guilt for something I'd done in childhood or my teens but didn't know what, and guilt now for hurting the people I loved.

I sat on the floor in front of the sliding glass door; cold air seeped in, around and under it. The concrete patio looked like a deep, black lake and the blurred lights were boats trapped in the darkness, lost, unable to find their way home. Like me. Cold. Alone.

Kevin's mother was probably setting the turkey on the table and my children and their cousins were taking their places at the children's table. The house smelled of baked turkey, sweet potatoes, pumpkin spice, and cinnamon. Presents were piled under the tree, and the multi-colored lights glowed. They didn't miss me, but I knew they all hurt for Kevin. He was a good man from a good family who did not deserve what I did to them.

I touched the ornaments on the tiny but real tree Brett, Kelli, and I had picked out—the construction paper, lace, and cotton ones they had made and the old ones Mom had given to me that, at one time, had hung on her tree.

I couldn't sit there any longer. I had to do something. I slipped into my raincoat, went outside, and walked in the cool, gentle rain. The dark was lit up by steady, twinkling lights glowing in windows, around eaves, and in the yards of neighboring houses. Plastic Santas and reindeer, swaying in the breeze, smiled at me. In front of many of the houses were several cars and in a couple of yards were manger scenes—Mary, Joseph, a cow, a lamb, and, of course, baby Jesus. Tomorrow I'd retrieve my children and go to my parents' home, where everything would be normal, and I'd fake Christmas spirit. Again.

The raindrops began to fall a little faster. My hair stuck to my head, dropping water into my eyes and face. I kept walking. My mind carried me back to the first time I'd felt this way during the holidays. It was raining then, too.

It was my second Christmas without Dad. Last year Mom had come with me, but this year she dropped me off at the door.

"Don't you want to come with me?" I asked one last time as I opened my car door.

"It was a bit awkward last year," she explained. "Besides, I'm sure your dad will be here this year. He loves his family and these get-togethers. And he loves you even more."

I wasn't so sure.

"Give Nana Scott a big hug from me and tell her I'll always love her."

"Why don't you tell her yourself?"

She reached across the seat and said, "I love you," as she shut the car door and drove away, leaving me standing in the rain.

Before I got to the front door, Nana Scott rushed out to me with an umbrella, hurrying me inside while hugging me.

It was the same as always. The air inside was warm and moist with the same holiday scents, baking turkey, pumpkin spice, cinnamon, apples, and peppermint. The adults I loved, and who loved me, were in little groups talking as if each group were competing for all the rooms' air and sound waves. My aunts hugged me, like always, and my uncles gave me a pat on the head. I played with my cousins and we snuck cookies shaped like Christmas trees and presents and Santa Claus away from the kitchen counter. At dinnertime, we sat at the small kids table next to the long adult table. Uncle Mike thanked God for our blessings and carved the turkey. The same as always.

But nothing was the same to me. I felt alone. Out of place. I didn't belong here or anywhere else. Looking back, it's easy for me to understand what I should have thought and felt. Then, however, all I knew was that something was wrong or missing and it was somehow my fault. The day he left, Dad was mad and had screamed at Mom and me. He did that a lot, but he always came back. Except that time.

Since then, he hadn't come to see me. He hadn't called or even sent a card for my twelfth birthday. I missed him. He'd taught me to throw and bat a softball and run the bases. Mom, Dad, and I used to go on picnics and swimming. Together. Why did he leave? Why didn't he come to see me?

Did I do something awful? I talked back sometimes and snuck out at night when I wasn't supposed to. But that was it.

I'd asked Mom and the only answer she ever gave me was, "I don't know."

While Uncle Mike passed out the presents, I watched the front door, knowing that at any minute it would burst open and Dad would run in. It was the only present I wanted. I'd drawn a picture, written, and mailed the invitation myself. He didn't answer it, but I figured if he for some reason couldn't come, at least he'd send me a gift or call, something to say he remembered me. As I opened gifts, I examined each card carefully and tried to conceal my disappointment. I should've been excited and grateful to get a silver bracelet, a dark blue V-neck sweater, and a new Barbie with clothes and a bathtub. I said thank you, but I didn't mean it. I wanted to go home, get in bed, and cry.

After everyone left, Nana Scott and I sat on the couch surrounded by remnants of the party: wrapping paper and ribbons, soggy green paper plates with melted vanilla ice cream and mushy chocolate cake, and red cups with water trickling down the sides, all on the coffee table and end tables without coasters. She slipped her arms around me, held me, and let me cry.

"You know your dad loves you," she said.

"Who cares? I don't."

Nana Scott knew it was a lie. Deep inside me, I knew it too, but couldn't admit it—even to myself.

She patted my knee, pushed me away, and said, "Go look on the kitchen counter. You've got one more present."

I sprinted to the kitchen, picked up the red package with its bright golden ribbon as if I'd found the Holy Grail, and ran back to the living room to show her. She shook her head. "No, it's not from your dad," she said. "This is my special gift for you."

Instantly, I deflated and lost interest in whatever it was but opened it anyway. It was a pale blue jewelry box with a ballerina that spun slowly around and played "Raindrops Keep Falling on my Head," an old song Dad sang to me when I was little and upset about something—the same song Nana Scott had sung to him.

"I know it's hard to understand now," she said as she patted my hand. "He does love you, but he never grew up. He thinks he's a man, but he's still in that toddler stage where the world revolves around him."

I didn't mean to, but the words just blurted out of my mouth, "I'm not a part of his world? He can't find two hours for me? What's wrong with me?"

"If you don't remember anything else I've tried to teach you, I want you to remember this. . ." She placed her palms on my cheeks and gazed directly into my eyes. "There is nothing wrong with you. It's him. When you're feeling sad and depressed, I want you to open this jewelry box and remember how special and strong you are. You're like this little ballerina who never gives up...you keep on dancing."

That night, when everyone else was asleep, I sat beside my bedroom window and stared at the driveway, opening and reopening the jewelry box, silently singing the words, "Raindrops keep falling on my head. . ."

I got back to the house, shrugged off my raincoat, and found the little jewelry box on the dresser where I had kept it through many moves and changes. I opened it and just as it always did, even after all these years, the box played "Raindrops keep falling on my head. . ." I felt Nana Scott's arms around me and heard her voice: "You're special and strong." I put on my dancing shoes and kept going.

Tuesday at the Mall

Mike Wahl

Without thinking, I held open the door for the woman who had approached the mall entrance at the same time so she could enter first. It was the way I had been raised, but not necessarily the present politically correct reaction. My thoughts had been focused on how I could possibly endure the next ten hours of sitting in Santa Claus' seat. Today's kids were largely a greedy lot, with their minds centered on all the worldly possessions they were requesting. The parents were to blame, unable to separate themselves from the god of prosperity, their children automatically imitated their mentors. I was always more embittered from these encounters, when Santa's hours were over, than from any other disappointments of the day.

She had three kids with her, carrying the youngest so he wouldn't slow her determined pace. Sneering at me, and ignoring the open door, she opened the adjoining door herself and shooed her brood inside. They obviously had a lot of shopping to do with only two days left before Christmas. I jostled back into the reality of false impressions, found it easy to be thankful that this temporary job would soon be over. How had some females become so preoccupied with themselves that they thought every action was an insult to their capabilities, no matter how innocent the intent? I was soon changed from my civilian clothes into the disguising red and white garb that marked me as an ambassador from the North Pole.

There had only been one bright spot during the first four hours before Santa's lunchtime. A girl in her early teenage years, who was old enough to have learned Santa's truth, stood in line for fifteen minutes just for the chance to tell me that all she wanted for Christmas were books. Books? That's all? Bless you, my child! Her name was Leah. I wanted to hug her, but propriety prevented that. I could only hope my own daughter would have made the same request.

On my way back to *the* chair after lunch, I had to walk past the line of excited kids waiting for Santa's return "from feeding the reindeer." Predictably, the line had grown quite long, and I greeted my future guests with rounds of gusty "HO! HO! HO!" and "Merry Christmas!" About half-way along, there she was, with her three kids waving wildly at Santa. She looked worn out from shopping, burdened by packages that Santa could have delivered easily, but she didn't know the real me. When it was their turn for photos with Santa, an elf surreptitiously supplied me with the three names of my next visitors.

The youngest, Noah, around age two, who had previously been exuberant when waiting in line, had now become hesitant about sitting on a stranger's lap. Who could blame him, though, as it went against everything he had been taught. Mama would have none of it. After all of that shopping and standing in line, that child WAS going to have his picture taken with Santa, no matter what! Noah's brother and sister begged and coaxed him to join them next to Santa. He just cried louder and clutched tighter to mama's pants leg. She unclasped the tiny hands, hoisted him upwards, and propelled them both towards the narrow space of lap between brother and sister, where she plopped the sobbing child.

With glee, she retreated from camera range, and loudly proclaimed that it would be a great picture. Last year, she said proudly, when it was Noah's first photo with Santa, he had smiled on cue, and this would be a great comparison. Of course, to her, that was all that mattered about Christmas. That once again, she had got *her* way, without regard to the feelings of anyone else. It must be the new true meaning of Christmas, overpowering the obsolete old way with tears of fear instead of joy.

Annie's Gift

Ann Nunnally

Annie scooted as close as she could to the brilliant silver package under the Christmas tree. "Don't touch it" she was told by her older brother, Prentiss. He was the bearer of the gift that would change Annie's life. She could still remember the night he walked into the living room with his girlfriend, Edna, and the most beautiful package she had ever seen. The silver wrapping paper with bold red stripes was as bright as a mirror and it seemed to be much longer than the two feet she later read on the box. In her mind, it was the biggest present she had ever seen in all of her seven years of life, and it had her name on it!

Prentiss and Edna smiled at one another as they considered her reaction to the present. They appeared to be pleased with their purchase and were anxious to watch Annie on Christmas day as she opened her surprise.

Being careful not to touch the gift of love, Annie changed positions in order to consider the treasure from another perspective. The raw wooded floor, the chill in the unheated house, and the smell of turnip greens cooking and sweet potatoes baking could not distract her from the dreams of Christmas morning. What could possibly be in this giant box with her name on it?

All Annie knew of Christmas was the gift baskets filled with groceries and delivered by local churches to the needy at Christmas. Her family was evidently on several lists of the poor and disadvantaged because they always received two or three baskets during the holidays. Annie always helped her mom shop for socks and underwear, wrapped them, including her own, and put them under the tree for Christmas morn. She would walk to the Piggly Wiggly with her mom and search for a big fat chicken for the cornbread dressing that would make Christmas dinner stellar. That was about the extent of Annie's Christmas experience...except the trip last year to meet a character named Santa.

Annie and her mom had hopped on the city bus in their quest to find Santa. After walking the streets of downtown Tuscaloosa for what seemed like an eternity, they rounded the corner at Brown's Department Store and there he was. Perhaps it was the loud "Ho, Ho, Ho!" or the size of the large, white bearded man in a red suit that made Annie freeze. She was motionless and big crocodile tears began to form in the corners of her eyes. Annie grabbed her mother's skirt and buried her face so the loud, red giant was not in sight. She could hear her mother's laughter as her tears began to fall profusely and her whole body trembled in fear. Annie had not understood the concept of Santa Claus. There had been no daddy in the home to represent Santa and no presents as a reward for her being good. She was totally ignorant and unprepared for this encounter. Her mother would laughingly tell the story over and over again through the years about Annie's first chance meeting with Santa. *No matter,* Annie thought as she looked once again at the silver wrapped box with her name on it. *Who needs Santa?*

The Christmas tree sheltering the special gift was beautiful to Annie. In the evening she would lay down on the floor in front of the tree and look at every light. It was magical.

The lights were a source of anger for Annie's mother. They had been a January 1st birthday gift to Annie from her grandmother. Sure, they were used, scratched, and still warm from grandmother's Christmas tree but they would be lights for all the upcoming years and Annie was willing to wait. The hand-me-down lights were better than no lights at all. Their glow made the wrinkled, repeatedly used tinsel dance with colors.

Annie loved Christmas! She was untouched by the poverty, dysfunctional family, offense, and unforgiveness that those around her seemed to wear as a Christmas garment.

The year prior, Annie began to attend services at the little Baptist church down the road. She had been invited to join a church group for young girls and some of her elementary school friends were attending. She walked by herself to all the meetings—no one else in her family attended.

In church, she heard the real story of Christmas. Annie was amazed when she learned of God's great love for mankind and of the baby born in Bethlehem, announced by the angels, who came to die for the sins of the world. His mother, Mary, and father, Joseph, had agreed to be a part of God's plan for redemption. Annie thought, *They must have really loved God. I want to love God, too.*

Taking one last look at the silver and red gift under the tree, Annie smiled and thought "Only two more days until Christmas."

She made her way to the kitchen where her mom had boiled some hot water on the stove, cooled it down by adding cold water, and had prepared a bath for Annie in a galvanized tub. It felt good, and Annie would go to bed clean and ready for a good night's sleep. As she dried herself off with the squeezed-out washrag, she thought, *When I awake there will only be two more days before I can open my special gift.*

The days passed quickly and Christmas morning came with the fury of preparing food and waiting for family to arrive so the presents could be opened. As Annie finally opened the large silver and red striped present, her eyes almost popped out of her head. It was the most beautiful bride doll she had ever seen! A pearl tiara and veil, and a full-length lace gown clothed a charming, yet friendly faced, two-foot-tall doll. Her dark, curled hair, perfect complexion, crystal blue eyes, and geranium pink lips were perfect. Annie never imaged something so beautiful and extravagant could be hers. She hugged the most beautiful gift she had ever received. It was hers. It wasn't a hand-me-down. It was expensive, and it would be an example of hope and womanhood for Annie to aspire to. She named her Bonnie.

Bonnie would stay by Annie's side throughout the turbulent teen years. Physical abuse, emotional abuse, and almost constant terror could all be soothed in the arms of Bonnie. She understood, never said harsh words, and comprehended the tears. Bonnie listened to what was too painful to tell others. Bonnie remained beautiful through the years and reminded Annie that she would be a beautiful bride one day. She was a companion, a secure place, and a home of hope.

The summer before Annie started her freshman year in high school, the unthinkable happened. The years of domestic violence, uncertainty, poverty, and alcoholism culminated in the death of Annie's grandfather at the hands of her father. The years of praying for change, a real daddy, salvation, and restoration of the family ended. The humiliation was epic as the murder became front-page news just weeks before school started. Enough tears to flood a city gushed from all the family members and only Bonnie remained stable and tangible at Annie's side.

Through Annie's faith and the unmerited grace of God, the storm passed and life, although forever changed, continued. High school days were filled with friends, adventures, a greater love and understanding of God's word, and a growing hope for a great future. Annie learned that her life could be the sum of wise choices she made and not the creation of poor choices others before her had made. Through it all, Annie always loved Christmas and the truth that "God so loved that He gave..."

At the end of high school, Annie packed up her belongings, although very few, and moved into the honors dorm at the University of Alabama. God had provided a full scholarship for her continued education. When her half of the dorm room was set up, her twin bed was covered in a homemade bedspread, a pillow, and Bonnie. Annie and Bonnie both attended college, dated, and got married twelve years after the large silver box was opened that Christmas day in 1958.

Christmas for Annie was more than the desperate circumstances of life. It was the gift of Bonnie. It was the gift of God's son, born in humble beginnings in a stable so He might understand Annie in her humble beginnings. It was "God with us…Immanuel." Christmas had always been and always would be beautiful.

Bonnie was irreparably damaged in a move to another city and state. It was a devastating experience for Annie. The death of her closest friend. Bonnie still lives in Annie's heart and comforts during difficult times. She is a forever memory of hope and God's faithfulness.

Likewise, Jesus lives forever in Annie's heart and mind, and always listens to the good and the bad life serves up. He is a forever gift of love, joy, and peace.

By now you have probably guessed that I am Annie. Some of my closest friends still call me Annie, but to the world I am "Pastor Ann," "Dr. Ann," or "Sister Ann." To my sons, daughters, and grandchildren, I am "Mom" or "Meena." To my husband, that Bonnie approved, I am "Sweetheart" and have been for past fifty years.

I have found through the years that Christmas is very rarely "picture perfect." As a child, I thought I was the only one with a father in prison, government food supplements, unpaid rent, hand-me-downs for clothes, harsh words, abusive parents, and heartbreak. Now I know that millions of families suffer through "the most wonderful time of the year." I find joy in sharing gifts to children like Annie, hope to families destroyed by drugs and alcohol, and the good news of the Bethlehem babe who would become the Savior of the world.

As Luck Would Have It

Laura Hunter

Darkness crept under the tree canopy as Willard Peeples forced himself up the incline. He had left the road half an hour back and trudged up the mountain trail heading home. The longer he hiked, the shallower his breath became. After walking two hours from Fort Payne, he was convinced that the mountain would kill him. Some coyote would find him face-down in leaves moldered from recent December rain.

A sharp pain cut under his left ribcage without warning. He forced himself to sit, to rest until his breath eased.

He could lessen his load by leaving the backpack where it now lay and move on empty-handed, but that would negate his journey. The Christmas toys, small as they were, were meant for his two girls April and June. His wife Caroline had had a spitting fit when she came to after each birthing and read the names on the birth certificates. He chuckled at the memory. She had wanted each to be named after her mother. He had named them for the months in which they were born "to help them remember their birthdays," he had said, "if I can't give them a real party."

He wished he had had enough money to buy something nice for Caroline, but after his arrest she would have accused him of stealing whatever he brought her.

Willard had first heard about early release for non-violent prisoners on the exercise yard. Goliath, a prisoner whose name fit his size, sat down by Willard and eyed the tower guard. "You and me gonna be catching the chain soon. Getting out of here, man," he whispered.

"Yeah" Willard spoke with his back to the tower. "Like we're growing wings and fly." He snorted.

"Duck, that fresh guard, he ain't no bug. He say cell warriors being released 'fore the virus kill us all."

Willard straightened his back. "You calling me a cell warrior?"

"Reckon you are. You mouth off in the house, then come out here in the yard standing all by yourself waiting for somebody to Molly whop your ass. Knowing all the time you ain't gonna hit back. Shoot, man, ain't your fault you a 'sweet kid.'"

"I ain't no fighter, that's all." Willard broke off a weed growing between a concrete square and the wall and chewed on the stem. "Why they letting us go?"

"They ain't room to separate us who's getting sick and, black market's run masks up so high they can't buy for ever-body. So they's giving us gate money and setting us free. Don't never have to come back."

"Believe it when I see it," Willard countered.

Goliath gave Willard time to digest what he had told him. When Willard said no more, Goliath picked him for information.

"Heard you in for fencing."

"Naw. Robbery first degree."

"Can't see you with no weapon,"

"Had my hunting knife in my pocket. Got me five years."

"What'd you steal, some old lady's lap dog?" Goliath grinned out the side of his mouth.

"Meat. Had me a good plan. Worked a couple of times. Just run out of luck, I guess."

"How so?"

"Go in a busy grocery. One of them big ones. Fake a limp and get in one of them electric carts. You got on baggy jacket and pants, see. Drive 'round abouts like you looking for something then go to whatever it is you want. Stuff what you want in your clothes. Sleeves is best. Drive out following some old woman who's got her arms full like you belong with her. That's all there is to it. You can even leave the cart in the lot. They don't expect a crip to walk it back in."

"Why'd you waste your time on meat? Why not beer? Liquor? Something good?"

"The wife and kids was hungry. Been laid off work for a couple of months when I first tried it. It worked that time and the next. But on the third time, some sassy teenager with a swinging ponytail followed me out and got my tag and turned me in. Cops stopped me 'fore I got out of the parking lot."

"That ain't fair. Stealing meat 'cause your wife and babies is hungry? And you didn't even pull your shank? How'd they reckon with that?"

"Had two DUIs with resisting arrests. Third strike in this state. Three strikes and you're out. Well, you're in. In the big house. So here I sit talking to a giant Black man who's weaving some tall tale 'bout getting out of here. Humph."

Goliath nodded. "Yep," he said and laughed.

"Man ain't no man less he can take care of his own," Willard said.

Christmas Eve three weeks later, Willard found himself locked out of the only home he had known for the past two years: Corrections Department Community, Atmore, Alabama. He had a bus ticket to Fort Payne. That was as close as a bus came to Sylvania. He had a twenty-dollar bill the State allotted him and one mask in his pocket. The other mask he wore over his nose and mouth. He had come to believe what Goliath had told him about the dangers of ignoring the virus, with prisoners dying like dogs in a rigged fight. He kept the second mask folded and pressed so he could give it to Caroline if she needed it to go someplace public.

Goliath stayed behind in the infirmary, bedded down, trying to suck in air against the pandemic that was spreading across the world as fast as people could breathe.

Willard boarded the Greyhound bus. He ought to arrive by 8 p.m., walk the rest of the way up Sand Mountain and give his girls their presents by Christmas Day. He slinked to the back of the bus, eyeing passengers in masks who watched as he passed by and shuttering as he passed men with no masks in sight. They ought to have been in with him and seen the lines of bodies who got the back door parole. He sensed each of the scattered passengers knew by his worn jacket and his Bo Bos, as they called their white prison tennis shoes, that he had just been released. He might as well have had the tat "ex-con" on his forehead.

By the time the bus pulled into Fort Payne, Willard's gut growled against being empty all day. He needed food, but first he had to buy presents for his girls. Twenty dollars wouldn't buy much, he knew. He walked north toward the mountain. Throughout town, boarded windows startled him. The place looked like it expected a tornado or hurricane to blast it off the map. He met not a single person. Not even a stray dog roamed the streets. The town was shuttered and locked. Everything appeared so different. In comparison, the prison community could have existed on a different planet. Fear danced before him, daring him to breathe easy and walk straight. He could do neither.

He pushed himself forward recalling the softness of his girls' hair and how his wife's body felt against his chest as he lay with her. These memories helped stave off hunger that had set his hands to trembling. In the distance he saw lights of a Dollar General. He knew from his time before prison that the word "Dollar" lied. Nothing in the store sold for only a dollar, but items weren't as expensive as those in a large department store. Not that department stores were a choice. They were nailed up with plywood boards.

Overhead, Christmas lights blinked from an irregular electricity source and reflected garish colors in street puddles. After living under lighted prison yards, Willard didn't recall nights being so dark—even with puny lights crossing each street. Late December drizzle wet Willard's hair, weather typical of an Alabama Christmas, overcast and damp. He noticed how cold he had become when he opened the store's door. Heat curved around him like a large snake and sent a shiver through his body. He stepped aside to disappear among the shelves.

His running nose reminded him that he wore his mask. No one would be able to identify him, even if he did something out of place. He pinched his nose and the mask absorbed his snot. He smiled and wondered if a woman approaching him saw the joy in his eyes. She walked away from him and said, "Social distancing, young man. Social distancing." Her tone reprimanded him. He'd not heard of this social distancing. In prison, he had been aware of anyone behind him to prevent his back from being stabbed. They called it "dancing on the blacktop," not some fancy name like "social distancing." He noticed what other customers did and followed suit. They avoided each other as if each had a plague.

He found the toy aisle. Skipping the boys' section, he centered on the girls. He hoped to find two pretty dolls with curls and dresses with lace. Maybe even find tiny shoes and socks. Within a minute, he stood before the dolls. Two of the prettiest dolls he had ever seen, one dressed in green and another in scarlet. Both were perfect for Christmas. He picked one up. A stocker called out to him, "Don't touch it if you don't plan to buy it." Startled, he replaced the doll. Beneath where the dolls stood was their price: $39.00 each. Willard backed away as if the price spit venom. He could never pay that, not with a twenty in his pocket. He glanced around as if trying to decide on other toys. No one was watching. He could pocket the dolls and walk right out. But Caroline would know when she saw his face that he had stolen the dolls. He walked down the aisle to find something he could afford.

Near the end of the aisle, he found a bin of stuffed toys. Tiny toys that looked more like baby toys than toys for girls six and seven. But the sign drew him in: "$5 each." Two toys for ten dollars and ten dollars left for Caroline. Forget food. He'd pocket a candy bar on the way out. Rummaging through the bin, Willard chose a pink unicorn with a glittery, purple mane and a purple tail. It was no larger than the palm of his hand, but it was cute, little-girl-cute. The second one he chose was a two-tone green turtle about the size of the unicorn. He approached the counter to pay when he remembered Caroline.

Caroline didn't care for anything frivolous. She didn't want fancy clothes. He walked past the knick-knack aisle, past the tee-shirt racks and turned into the necessities aisle. An older woman in a red woolen coat stood in the middle of the aisle leaning on a black cane. She turned a box that contained masks over and over. The price beneath the boxes stated "6 for $10." He was certain that Caroline had no masks. Not out where they lived. A box of six would give two for the three of them. He could continue to use his and, if Lloyd was still in the house, he could share his extra with his father-in-law. The masks and stuffed toys were the perfect gifts, and he would have paid for all of them on his own. He walked lighter to the register.

The woman in the red coat checked out, buying four boxes. A loud-mouthed man behind Willard said, "You ain't supposed to hoard, Lady." The woman ignored him and moved on.

Willard watched the dark-haired teenager at the register. Her mask moved back and forth as she chewed her gum. He put his three items on the counter. She looked over her mask and said, "That all?"

"Yep." Willard would have rocked back and forth on his toes with delight had he not been afraid he would attract attention.

The register dinged. "Twenty-two dollars," the girl said.

Willard hesitated to speak. When he did, he stumbled over his words. "The prices say five dollars for each toy and ten dollars for the masks. Where you get twenty-two dollars?" He had to concentrate not to raise his voice. Goliath had warned him not to make himself obvious. "Don't nobody trust a ex-con," he had said.

"Tax," she said. "Ten percent. That's two dollars. Want to put something back?"

The whole scene was so ridiculous that Willard waited for her to blow a bubble through her mask.

The loud-mouthed man laughed. "You just crawl out from under some rock? City increased tax a good year ago."

"Hush, James. Maybe he ain't from 'round here," his wife said.

Willard cringed. The line behind him, although they were several feet away, had heard everything that had been said. In a sprint of frustration, he shoved the box of masks aside and said, "Here. How much for the toys?"

The girl sighed as if she had been asked to perform a calculus equation. She clicked her cash register keys and chewed out the words, "Eleven dollars." Her gum cracked behind her mask. "Now. That it?"

"Yeah." Willard's hands fluttered as if they'd lost track of what they should be doing. The store's heat had closed in on him, and Willard wiped sweat from his brow.

The girl counted out nine dollars and slapped them into Willard's palm. Willard balled the money and stuffed it in his pants pocket.

Outside the store, the woman in a red coat leaned on her cane and struggled with opening the passenger door of her BMW while holding her sack of masks. Willard had been here before—when people who needed less took more and when he, who needed more, had to settle for less or sometimes settle for nothing. Willard's anger vaulted through his body and erupted from his arms and legs. He kicked her cane. It clattered on the sidewalk. She fell. He grabbed her sack of masks and ran.

Hidden between two cars, she said "Help me" in a tiny voice that expected no response.

Willard tossed his and her sack behind a trash can around the corner and walked back as if he had just appeared. He stepped between the cars to help her up. There lay her purse, open, with contents spilled about. He stooped and picked up a lipstick, a comb, and a wallet. He put the lipstick and comb back in her purse and handed it to her as he lifted her off the concrete. With her back to him, he slid her wallet into his back pocket without thought.

"You alright?" he said.

"I'm okay. Can you reach my cane? Some man grabbed my sack and ran with it. Did you see him?"

"No. I come from the other direction. Didn't see nobody." He handed her cane to her and helped her up the curb.

"Thank you. You have a good Christmas."

"Yes, ma'am. You, too." If he'd had a cap, he would have tipped it to prove he was a gentleman. Willard sidled down the sidewalk, stooped down, and picked up the sacks. He turned north. If he walked at a good clip, he could get home before the girls were asleep.

The trudge up the mountainside grew harder. Willard coughed a dry cough from time to time. He stopped again to rest, but the longer he sat on the damp ground the colder he became. Clouds had hidden the moon, so he had little idea how late it had become. Worried that April and June would be in bed when he arrived, he walked faster. Up the road, he rounded the last bend.

There it was, the plank house where he had grown up, where his wife and girls waited for him. Smoke coiled out of the chimney as air flattened it against its escape. Low pressure meant a cold, cold morning. Caroline had created a wreath for the door. She had wired pine boughs together and woven a strip of burlap through the needles to make it look festive, to look like more than dying branches tacked to wood.

It was good to be home again.

He took the toys out of his backpack and put them into his back pants pockets. So he wouldn't wake the girls if they slept, he gave the door his slightest tap. The door swung open so fast Willard thought somebody had been waiting on the other side. The room smelled like dry ash, as if the hearth had not been cleaned in weeks. Before him stood Lloyd. His father-in-law had changed little. He wore his thick work shirt and pants, both khaki and stiff, and his dirty steel-toed shoes. His hair fell forward, now gray around his ears.

"Well, it's the thief come home wearing his mask."

"Howdy, Lloyd," Willard said. "Girls still up?"

Lloyd moved aside.

There they stood, each barefoot, dressed in a nylon gown. Caroline had a thick green sweater over her gown and an arm around each child. Each girl wore one of Willard's plaid flannel shirts. Light from the fireplace cast a glow behind them.

Willard reached out to them. The children waited. "Never saw no prettier girls in all my life." He laughed. "Come here and give me a hug."

"What're you doing with that mask?" Caroline said. Willard coughed into his elbow. Caroline pulled down the mask and kissed him hard on the mouth. "Why didn't you tell a body you was coming home?"

Both girls screamed, "Daddy!" They ran and grabbed his thighs.

Lloyd sat in a chair by the fireplace, watching the reunion, a scowl on his face.

"Can you believe it?" Willard said. "I was walking up the road and who did I meet but Santy Claus his own self. And he says, 'You going to see them Peeples girls?' and I says, 'I reckon I am,' and he says 'Take them these toys for me,' and he reaches in his bag and pulls out..." He brought the stuffed toys from behind him and offered them to the girls, a toy in each hand.

The girls squealed.

Lloyd grunted. "Why'd you bring some baby toy?"

"Shut up, Daddy," Caroline said. She cradled Willard close, her arm around his waist.

Willard took a box of masks from the bag and handed it toward Caroline. "Here, we'll be needing these masks."

Caroline reached for the box and the bag.

"Masks?" Lloyd shouted. "What kind of present is that? Some fool's filled your head with nonsense about some sickness we can't see. Can't smell it. Can't taste it. Ain't real, I say." He stepped forward. "Just like that man they say walked on the moon when they was out in Arizona filming." He thrust out his chest. "And I say what I know. And I know you a no-count father and a no-count husband." Lloyd beat Caroline to the sack and flung it in the fire.

Willard jumped toward the fire and grasped for the bag, but it had landed on the hot logs. The plastic curled as it melted; the boxes inside, blazed. Willard came at Lloyd, punching the air, kicking. He picked up the nearest slat-bottomed chair and hurled it at Lloyd. It missed.

Lloyd rose from his duck and balled his fist as if to hit Willard. Willard bent and head-butted Lloyd. Lloyd fell, his head landing with a deep thud on the rock hearth. He didn't move.

April screamed.

June cried, "Grandpa!"

Caroline squatted over her father and tried to rouse him. "Daddy? Daddy?" she intoned.

April stripped off her daddy's flannel shirt and tucked it under her granddaddy's head to collect the blood.

"I ain't a fighter, Caroline, but he done burnt our masks and kilt us all." Willard covered his tears with his hands and, coughing, sat hard on the floor.

"You didn't go to do it, Baby," Caroline said.

Willard rocked back and forth. He grasped the one remaining box of masks from Caroline and held it to his chest as if embracing a frail child.

No Christmas Miracles

Peter Last

"Seven dollars."

Brian watched the woman extract a wad of bills from her bra and parse out three of the damp, limp pieces of paper. Two weeks ago, he would have shuddered at accepting the money, but in that time, thousands of bills had passed through his fingers, many of them wet, dirty, crumpled, crusty, or worse. God only knew how many diseases he had narrowly avoided up to this point. Or perhaps had contracted and simply was not showing symptoms yet.

"Good morning," the next customer said as he scribbled on a questionnaire. "How are you?"

"Tired."

Brian would have rubbed the sleep from his eyes, but he made a habit to never touch his face during his shift. Instead, he glanced at the clock which proudly displayed the time as a mere thirteen minutes past five.

"Don't I know it, man," the client chuckled. "Nothing like waking up at four thirty just to get in here before work. I reckon you must wake up even earlier."

"Four," Brian confirmed. He looked at the man to accept the seven one-dollar bills and was taken aback by what he saw. It was easy to assume everyone who came here was a drug addict complete with every stereotype imaginable. A couple weeks here had nearly confirmed the prejudice, but then along would come someone like this. A young man, early twenties, nice smile, suit and tie—not Brian's idea of a druggie.

"Well, thanks for opening early," the man said. "Not sure I could make it through the day without this."

Brian gave a small wave in acknowledgement and produced a sad smile as the man took a seat in the waiting area. It was easy to look down on those who were not like him, to think their sins were worse than his, but he was continually shown the error of his assumptions. Reprobates on the far end of the downhill journey with their health problems and criminal records made for good television commercials, but the opiate crisis was no respecter of persons, made more insidious by the fact addiction could start with a legal prescription. Once again, Brian thanked God for his good health—that he had never had to use powerful pain killers. There but for the grace of God, he would be as well.

"Seven dollars," he said, though the next customer already had the money out. He winced inwardly as he took the money. One of the bills was crusted with something he hoped was neither the result of a bodily fluid nor cocaine. It probably was not, he told himself. Then again, it wouldn't hurt to bring latex gloves to his next shift.

"This is wrong again."

Shelly's boss couldn't even wait until she was completely inside his office before telling her what she had done wrong.

"What do I need to fix?" Shelly asked in a detached tone. This was not the first time she had been called into Jack's office, nor would it be the last. Jack never looked away from his computer screen but waved a stapled report covered in red notations.

"Were my calculations wrong?" Shelly asked as she took the papers and flipped through them. "I'm pretty sure I was looking at the right references, though the whole set of regulations is so confusing I can't be one hundred percent sure."

"I'm sure all your numbers are correct, but the formatting is atrocious," Jack said. "Words need to be capitalized, oxford commas all over the place, and I counted at least thirteen times you didn't put two spaces after a period. This isn't hard to figure out. Why can't you get it straight?"

Because you don't follow the regulations and everyone in this godforsaken place has a different way they want to see my reports! Shelly thought bitterly. She left the office, report hanging limply by her side. The meeting was over.

"What did he say?" Jerry asked when Shelly returned to their shared cubical.

"Didn't like the formatting," Shelly grunted and tossed the papers onto her desk. "Either too lazy or too incompetent to know if the information is correct."

"Well, he is a lot more concerned with how it looks than what's in it," Jerry agreed. "What are you gonna do? Just make the changes so he's happy."

"Happy?" Shelly said. "He's never happy. I think the only time he enjoys himself is when he's marking up reports for stupid, pedantic reasons. You know he doesn't even use the writing guide? It's official guidance from Washington, and he ignores it!"

"So does everyone else here," Jerry pointed out. "I think sixth-grade English teachers run this place. It's their inerrant teaching which determines how people want things written, official guidance be damned. Just make the changes and send it back."

"I know." Shelly covered her face with her hands and sighed. "I just don't like how he thinks I'm incompetent. If I keep this up, he's going to fire me, and I can't afford for that to happen."

"These are government jobs we're talking about," Jerry replied. "You know as well as I do the only way you can get fired is to steal something or, I don't know, watch porn on your government computer. If incompetence were grounds for firing, most of the people here wouldn't have jobs. Besides, we both know you're not incompetent."

Great, so my job is secure, Shelly thought as she turned to correcting the report. *The good news is I can continue to work in a job I hate for a boss who makes it a living nightmare all to keep up with the payments for property we can't afford.*

"Seven dollars." *Still, after all this time?* Brian's inner voice snarked.

The monotony of the day was interrupted, never a good thing in this vocation, by raised voices from outside. Brian continued to accept payments but craned his neck to look out the windows in the front of the building.

"Brian." Tom, the office's security guard was suddenly there. "Lock the door behind me and call the police."

Brian hurried around the desk into the waiting area and followed Tom to the door. The old, grey-haired man took a deep breath and stepped through the door, armed with nothing but his badge and some pepper spray. *It did not look good for him if bullets started flying*, Brian thought as he spun the door lock. *Then again, Tom had served in the first Gulf War, hadn't he? Perhaps he could hold his own, even without a weapon.*

The scene outside did not look bad yet, but things like this could go from innocuous to horrible in seconds. Two of the clients were yelling at each other over a fender bender by the looks of it. Brian remembered the police and fished his phone from his pocket as one of the people pushed the other. Tom started to run as they tussled, then a glint appeared in the sunlight followed by a sharp crack.

"911, what is your emergency?" the phone asked as Brian dove to the floor. He dropped it and it clattered across the tiles, sliding as he scrambled to retrieve it.

"Hello, hello?" he shouted into it when he had finally fumbled it to his ear.

"Yes, I'm here, sir," the dispatcher answered. "What is the nature of your emergency?"

"There's two guys fighting outside," Brian stammered. "At least one of them has a gun. He's fired it once." He winced at a second crack. "Twice now."

"Where are you located?" the dispatcher asked calmly. *Too calmly*, Brian thought as he gave the address.

"I've dispatched a unit," the dispatcher said after a moment. "They should be there in two minutes. Is anyone besides the two people you mentioned in immediate danger?"

"Our security guard, Tom, was trying to break up the fight," Brian answered. "He's still outside. Should I see if I can spot him?"

"No, stay away from the windows and get behind something solid," the dispatcher advised. "I'll let the officers know to look out for him. What does he look like?"

Another crack and Brian collapsed to the floor, dropping his phone a second time. This was definitely not worth eight dollars an hour.

"I want the parking lot closer to the building than that." The stars on the man's shoulders identified him as a general while the wings on his chest meant he knew nothing about facility designs. He probably didn't know much more than how to pull back on the stick to make the plane go up.

"I'm sorry, sir, but it's not possible to put the parking closer." Shelly tapped on the map where a colored line encircled the structure in question. "Regulations state that for force protection measures, we can't have vehicles getting closer to the building than here."

"I want my parking spot here," the general said as though Shelly had never spoken. He stabbed a bony finger toward the table, practically touching the building on the map.

It's for the house, Shelly reminded herself. *I put up with people like this so we can have the house and property.*

She abandoned the biting response first to her lips. "The closest I can put it is over here," she said instead.

"That's on the opposite side of the building from my office," the general snapped. "Unacceptable! I can't be expected to walk that far every day!"

You expect all your people to walk further than that, Shelly thought. She opted for the more tactful, "I'll get it as close as I can, sir, but there are regulations to follow."

"There is, of course, a waiver for everything, sir," Jack spoke up. "I'm sure it wouldn't be hard to get one for you."

Right, because explosions don't affect generals' offices as much as they do the rest of a building, Shelly thought bitterly. *Well, if the moron wants to get blown up for the sake of not having to walk so far, so be it, but I for one will not be doing the stupid waiver.*

"Shelly has done these waivers before," Jack said. "She got one pushed through for the medical clinic. This one shouldn't be a problem."

"That wasn't a waiver, Jack." Shelly struggled to keep her tone respectful. "Ambulances are required to be able to drive up to the building. It's in the reg."

"Well, I'm sure you'll figure this one out," Jack said with a dismissive wave of his hand.

"Good," the general declared as if him getting his way had ever been in question. "Now on the inside, I noticed my office does not have a kitchen attached to it."

Shelly opened her notebook and pulled out a pen. Taking notes gave her something to do besides throwing objects at the man before her.

The pace today was ridiculous. Why were so many people coming here on this day of all days?

"A number two, medium with a coke, a four-piece nugget, and a small fry. Will that be all?" Brian spoke to his headset. The bun for the sandwich was already in the toaster, and he tossed nuggets into a small box. "Your total will be $14.76. Please pull around to the first window."

The public seemed to have a craving for fast food today and it had been nonstop since the beginning of his shift. Cars crowded the drive-thru, looping the building, while a dozen families waited to place their orders at the front counter. The clock declared it was a mere three hours until Brian's shift ended and already his feet were dragging.

It's for the house. This had become Brian's mantra to get him through most days.

It's not even that nice of a house, an inner voice argued.

Sure, it needs some work, but I've never been afraid of that. Besides, it's not the house but the potential we bought. We can do anything we want with it. Animals, camping, gardening. Maybe even have our own business someday.

The inner voice did not rebut. It didn't have to. Instead, Brian's headset beeped in his ear, and he took a brief moment to compose himself before speaking.

"What can I get for you today?"

This person didn't know what they wanted, and Brian suffered through the whole ordeal, asking questions now and then, but mostly making the other orders which constantly flooded onto the screen above the prep table. When the customer finally got their order straight, he scurried back to the register to key it in. The fries squealed to be pulled from the oil which he did before returning to packaging food. All the while, another customer droned in his ear about their need for unhealthy burgers and subpar shakes.

The chicken was beeping at him now, begging to be removed from the hot grease. Brian stole a glance at the clock. A mere two hours and fifty-seven minutes until the end of his shift. How he would survive that long, he did not know.

Shelly quickly packed her bag, keeping an eye on the clock. She was already an hour late but, as usual, Jack had given her a task with an unreasonable deadline. Even now, an email stood prepared on her desktop. She would send it on her way out the door so Jack would not know she had gone until it was too late.

"Good, I caught you before you left."

Shelly jumped at the words, turning to see her boss standing in the door to her cubical.

"I need this done by Monday morning." Jack extended a stapled set of papers through the door frame. As Shelly hesitantly took them, she got the distinct impression Jack thought entering the work area of his lowly peons was somehow beneath him.

"We don't have work tomorrow," Shelly reminded Jack. She thumbed through the paper so she didn't have to look at her boss.

"Take your computer home," Jack replied. "You have three days." He turned to leave. "Plenty of time."

There was no longer any reason to move quickly, and Shelly slowly packed up the rest of her things, adding her laptop to the bag, hating herself even as she did it. She and Brian got little enough time together as it was. She did not need to be taking work home with her.

The thirty-minute trip home had lighter than usual traffic, it was Christmas Eve after all, and Shelly's mind had time to wander, to fume, to gripe, and to hate.

Why did Jack, the insensitive prick, give her work to do over Christmas? Had he no heart? And what about Jerry? Why didn't he ever stay late? It wasn't fair that Jack didn't give him the same amount of work as Shelly. He never had to take work home with him!

But you know who is really to blame for this? Brian. He talked me into buying this property. I knew it was a bad idea, but he pressured me until I agreed. With the market the way it is now, we can't even afford to sell, and it's all Brian's fault!

But in her soul, Shelly knew this wasn't true. They both had concerns, had talked through them, prayed about it. The purchase was expensive, but with her and Brian's jobs, they should have been able to pay it off early. It wasn't Brian's fault he had been laid off. He'd even gone out and secured three jobs, all of them far beneath his education and intelligence level, to help make ends meet.

Gradually, Shelly's anger was replaced with shame and sadness—two staples of her life these days. She normally covered these emotions with a smile, but today there was nothing left. No fake happiness to spread over her true feelings.

She turned onto their dead-end road, normally dark save for two streetlights. The last few weeks, however, their few neighbors had decorated, and now strings of lights atop fences and a spotlighted creche illuminated the road.

The festivity of the ornaments should have lightened Shelly's mood, but they served as a juxtaposition to the darkness of Shelly and Brian's property. She worked overtime and he held down three jobs, leaving no time to decorate. No time for lights on the porch railing, no time for a wreath on the door, no time for Christmas cookies, no time to get gifts for each other, and no time for a tree. The few presents they had received from family via the mail were stacked unceremoniously on the living room floor near the fireplace.

Shelly sat in the car for several minutes after parking, staring at the dark house, tears falling into her lap. When she finally got out of her car, Brian's car door opened as well, startling her. Brian swiped at his face as he collected his things while Shelly waited for him.

"How are you?" Brian asked as they headed to the house. They both knew better than to ask about work.

Shelly was about to give the same answer she always did. The world expected her to proclaim that everything was fine, but that was a lie.

"Not good." The words were out of Shelly's mouth before she could stop them.

"Why?" Brian asked, mildly surprised. They had danced this ballet a thousand times, never deviating from the script until today.

"Why? Because I'm miserable," Shelly answered. She dropped her bag on the porch and sat heavily on the steps. "I work too hard at a job I hate for a terrible boss who makes me work overtime even though it's illegal." She grabbed papers from her bag and waved them. "He gave me work to do this weekend! Over Christmas! What kind of a horrible person does that? And I put up with it all so we can make payments on property we haven't even been able to use because we're too busy. Oh, and our money problems are wrecking our marriage."

She dropped her head into her hands, both ashamed and relieved at the outburst. She suspected Brian already knew she felt this way, but at least now she had said it. A moment later, she felt an arm around her shoulders and looked up in surprise. Brian was sitting beside her and hugging her, well sort of. Either way, the physical contact was more than she had received from him in over six months. He didn't say anything because there was nothing to say. He knew the situation as well as she did.

"I know how you feel," Brian finally said. "I hate that you feel so stuck in your job. I wish I could help, but I feel helpless. After all, I'm the one with an engineering degree, stuck working fast food and front desk at a clinic."

"That's not your fault," Shelly said, lifting her head to look at him.

"Knowing doesn't make me feel any better, especially when I see what it's doing to you," Brian said morosely. "I wish I could help more."

Silence fell once again. They both knew the facts, the truth, their feelings. They also knew there was nothing they could do to fix the problem. Words certainly would not.

"It's just not fair, you know," Shelly said dully. She leaned her head against Brian's shoulder. "This is supposed to be a happy time of year and look at us. Only two hours till Christmas and I don't think I've ever been more miserable."

Another minute of silence. Brian suddenly laughed, and Shelly looked up at him.

"What's so funny?"

"It just occurred to me that we're living out the real Christmas Eve, aren't we?" Brian said.

"What do you mean?" Shelly asked.

"The world is in a bad spot now, seems to be getting worse every day, but I don't think it's ever been more hopeless than the day before Jesus was born," Brian explained. "No matter how bad things get these days, we have hope now. Our situation seems pretty hopeless. I don't know how it can get better or at least, how we'll last long enough to see it get better. But in two hours, it's Christmas—a reminder of how Jesus came to help us when we couldn't help ourselves. Humanity's problems didn't vanish with his arrival, fand we'll still have our problems tomorrow. But Christmas reminds us we have hope, no matter how bad things may seem."

Shelly laid her head back on Brian's shoulder and put an arm around his waist, her heart a little lighter. Brian was right. They had not solved anything today, and tomorrow would be no different. But they had hope—a hope easily forgotten, especially in hard times, but a hope which never disappeared. No matter what happened, they had each other and they had hope.

Moonlight

M. E. Hubbs

The bright moon was not an ally as the two began their midnight decent from the mountain. Shadows of boulders, some as big as a house, cast an impenetrable darkness across parts of the trail. The trek down from the summit was difficult in daylight, but treacherous in the moonlight-dappled dark. They paused in the shadows. It was warm for December, and the damp chill was chased away by the heat and sweat of the hike. The boulder on which they leaned sent a pleasant coolness through the seat of their worn trousers.

"You sure this is a smart thing, Bill? The Cap'un will have our hides if'n we get caught. That idiot Gen'ral Bragg put out clear orders about this very thing."

"Jes' leave it to me, Newt. My cousin Jobe has got picket duty right on the creek. He says the boys in his comp'ny do it all the time. I'm gonna' have me some coffee for our Christmas breakfast tomorrow."

Bill cinched the neck of the tow sack in his fist a bit tighter and continued down the mountain. Newt tripped and cursed under his breath, then blew hot air into his hands to warm them. The sound of water reached their ears before they made out the thin line of trees that edged the creek. Bill threw up his arm and stopped Newt's pace. "Hold up. We's gettin' close," he whispered.

Bill cupped one hand around his mouth and whispered as loud as he could, "Hooty-hoo, hooty-hoo."

A faint "hooty-hoo" answered from fifty yards down the creek.

"Hooty-hooo! What kind of fool call is that, Bill?"

"When me and Jobe was growing up we used an owl call to keep track of one another when we were separated in the woods."

"Well it doan sound nuthin' like a real owl," Newt complained.

"Yep, but Jobe knowed it was me right off. I didn't have to call out his name."

Newt harrumped, sending out clouds of vapor from his breath, but said nothing.

Jobe materialized as if by magic in a patch of moonlight. "I heard y'all stumblin' around halfway up the mountain. I thought they was a whole reg'munt of ya comin'. You bring the tobacco you wanna' trade?"

Bill handed him the sack. Jobe jabbed his hand in and pulled out a fist full of shriveled stalk. "What's this? This ain't proper tobacco, this here is just stalks! You can't smoke these! It'll taste like dried cow chips!"

"Shhh. Not so loud Jobe! I don't wanna' trade good tobacca' to a Yank. I peeled all the leaf off some plants I stole from a feller's tobacca' barn. I already chewed the leaf. I recon the Yank will sniff the bag for the smell of cured tobbaca' but won't figure out its just stalks till later. By then I'll have my coffee."

Jobe considered for a moment. "The Coachman will be pretty hot when he finds out he's been cheated. Well, it doan matter. He tole me his reg'munt is moving outta' this valley soon, so I doan reckon we'll see him on picket duty again."

"The Coachman, who the heck is the Coachman?"

"A feller in an Illinois reg'munt, on picket duty right on the other side of the creek. He used to drive some rich man's coach in Chicago."

The trio moved quietly down to the creek bank and settled behind the trunk of a dead oak.

Jobe cupped his hands around his mouth and called, "Hey, Coachman!"

"Hey, Pig Farmer." A hoarse whisper responded from across the water.

"Now don't be shooting none, Yank. We's gonna come out in the moonlight so's you can see we ain't got no muskets."

"Come on out," he replied. "You know we have our own rules down here. No use shooting at each other if there's a trade to be made."

The three rebels eased from behind the tree. They strained to see into the blackness of the opposite shore.

Bill and Newt were in awe for a moment. Neither had been this close to a live Yankee, much less talked to one. Newt was barefoot. He lifted one foot and rubbed his itchy sole on the coarse wool of the opposite leg.

"So yall's is from Chicago? I reckon there's lots of sin in a big town like Chicago!" Bill had a hint of delight in his voice. "I'm from Alabama. I doan reckon I ever seen more than a hunnert folks in one place 'til I joined this Army."

"I didn't come down here to swap stories, Rebs. What I need is tobacco for my pipe. Are we trading or not?"

"Send the coffee over first, then we'll send the tobacca," Jobe instructed.

The Coachman produced a board from behind a tree. Two feet long, its end was whittled into a sharp prow. From his haversack he pulled a small cloth bag which he placed on the board. With a swift push, the board sliced through the water towards the opposite side of the creek. The little craft caught the current and headed further down steam than the Coachman expected. As it passed through the dappled moonlight it looked like a little man in a boat.

"Send my smoke back over on the plank," the Coachman demanded.

Bill handed the bag of coffee beans to Newt and replaced it with the sack of to-bacco stalks. Newt hefted the bag and squeezed until he felt the familiar shape of coffee beans. A smile spread slowly across his face. Bill squatted and gave the plank a shove. It produced a chevron of watery ripples that sparkled in the moonlight. The arms of the Coachman extended from the shadows and retrieved the board and sack, then disappeared with a flash of blue back into the darkness. His voice came from the blackness.

"Rebs, pass the word. Don't show yourselves to the pickets tomorrow night. There's a new regiment moving into our old camp. They'll be on picket here. They don't know the rules and they're liable to shoot you. Oh, and have a Merry Christmas, Rebs!"

"Happy Christmas to you and yours, Yank!" Jobe added.

Bill and Jobe listened to the Coachman scurry up the bank and through the bushes back to his picket post.

Bill smiled with the completion of the transaction. He savored the memory of a cup of hot coffee, a pleasure he had not known since the previous spring. They watched in the dim light as Newt untied the bag and dug his fingers in the sack. His eyes narrowed with suspicion as he pulled out a damp bean. He crunched it between his teeth, then spit it out in disgust and said, "These here coffee beans has already been boiled!"

Bill screwed up his face and said, "Dang it! I should'a knowed it. How coulda' fella be that mean and stingy?"

"On Christmas Eve to boot!" Newt added.

Bill snorted, "You can't never trust a lying, theavin' Yank."

Police Chief Billy

Christal Cooper

During Christmas of 1980, I learned so many things through one simple act of goodness. The three years previous we lived in Spangdahlem Air Force Base in Germany. We lived in the village, but my memories are almost blank. However, as a ten-year-old living in Bonaire, Georgia my memory bank became more reliable.

We lived in a mobile home out in the country on Willingham Drive. We could see our next-door neighbor's house—it was two-story and looked so nice. I thought that was the kind of house I'd like to live in when I get older.

My sister Tracy was twelve years old, and my brother Jody was two months shy of his third birthday. I remember when in Germany he quit breathing at our house in the German village. My parents rushed my baby brother to the emergency room of the hospital at Spangdalhem. It seemed that Jody was past that baby stage and was now a strong and healthy toddler.

My mother had tons of presents wrapped in different colors of paper—my sister's in one color and mine in the other. I don't remember the specific colors we had, but I'll just say my gifts were wrapped in green paper since green is my favorite color.

We got a real tree that year. I don't remember how exactly, but I imagine we all got in the car and my dad drove and we walked through the Christmas tree farm to pick out the tree we wanted. Then I imagine we came home and decorated the tree while listening to Christmas music or to the soundtrack of Christmas movies playing on television.

My parents purchased a spray can that you sprayed all over the Christmas tree to make it appear that the tree was covered in glittery snowflakes. This delighted me. What would Christmas be without snow? I don't even remember if it was snowing outside, but I do remember it was very cold.

I imagine my sister and I were captivated by the Christmas tree and its glittering snowflakes—each one different from all others. Just like humanity—not one of us alike.

Suddenly, the same thing that happened almost three years ago in Germany happened again to my brother Jody. He looked at our snowy Christmas tree and quit breathing. Once again, my parents rushed my little brother to the ER, this time at Robins Air Force Base, in Warner Robins, Georgia.

It was soon that we learned that the reason my brother momentarily quit breathing was because of the artificial snow coming from the spray paint can. My parents stripped that Christmas tree of all its decorations and threw it at a garbage dump miles from our mobile home.

I remember my dad walking us down the hospital hallway to the room where my mother was attending to my brother. He was happy despite being completely enclosed in a huge plastic bubble. It made me think of the John Travolta movie, *The Boy in the Plastic Bubble,* that my sister and I stayed up late to watch on TV. My brother was in that bubble but he was no John Travolta—he was my baby brother, which suddenly made things no longer a fantasy. I was suddenly grateful to be the receiver of a gift—my brother's life.

I remember our next-door neighbors Mr. Billy and Mrs. Sara Hunter. They had two children: a teenager, Donna, who I thought was a dream, and Bryan, who was about my sister's age and is now a police officer in Warner Robins, Georgia. Mr. Billy was the Police Chief of Warner Robins, Georgia.

Mr. Billy, who I like to call "Police Chief Billy," was handsome. He had brown hair, was tall, and always had a smile on his face. I don't remember what his voice sounded like, but I'm sure that it was a soothing sound.

The evening my parents brought my brother back from the hospital, there was a knock at our door. My dad in his blue robe answered the door to find Police Chief Billy gripping a freshly cut Christmas tree. I remember him displaying the Christmas tree like he was one of those models on *The Price Is Right*, showing us kids the view from every angle. This time was different though because we didn't have to guess how much it cost or pay for it—it was free.

Police Chief Billy died on August 28, 2012. I was surprised to find out that his funeral took place at the same Southern Baptist church where I met and married my husband.

I regret that I never let Police Chief Billy know how much I appreciated what he did for my family and myself. I could have contacted him somehow while I was in high school or in college, or even as a wife and mother living away from Warner Robins, Georgia.

But despite this, every Christmas the ten-year-old girl's little heart that is still present in this fifty-two-year-old woman's body is reminded, through the memory of Police Chief Billy, that in order to give, we must receive, and in order to receive, we must give. One can't exist without the other.

How to Peel an Orange

Bill King

I have a Christmas memory that happened more than fifty years ago but remains fresh in my mind today: the day my dad taught me how to perform a simple task that anyone can do. What he taught me that day was nothing complicated. It took no extraordinary amount of talent. In fact, anyone with two hands and a sharp knife can do what he did. In spite of those facts, I have never forgotten what he showed me that day and have used what I learned numerous times through the years. Perhaps the best part of all, it helps me remember my time spent with him.

I can't recall a single time when my dad and I went Christmas shopping together. I do fondly recall that each year, a week or two before Christmas, he and I visited the local fruit stand. We didn't get much at Christmas, but we always had fruit, candy, and nuts. The nuts were still in the shell and the candy always included a box of peppermint sticks—not the hard kind that looks like a shepherd's staff, but the soft straight sticks that came in a box that contained a couple of dozen and melted in my mouth like pure sugar—probably because they were pure sugar.

I have often heard that there is more than one way to skin a cat, but honestly, I can't recall ever skinning a cat in any way, and I'm not sure why you would. But I do know there is more than one way to skin an orange. The Christmas fruit we brought home always included oranges and every year I tried to dig my fingernails under the skin of one of those oranges so I could pull off the peeling piece by piece. But this year was different. As I went to bury my fingers into the orange's peel, dad said, "Let me show you something." He reached into his pants' pocket and pulled out his three-bladed Case knife. There was no telling what all he had cut with that knife, and I probably didn't want to know. He opened the smallest blade and used it to score my orange rind all the way around, making a circle. He cut just deep enough to pierce the rind but not enough to cut the flesh of the orange. Then he repeated the process two more times, moving over a little each time. He made three circles around the orange, creating six pieces of scored rind, then he easily peeled off each piece in a matter of seconds.

I actually can't remember for sure, but I think this may have been the last Christmas dad and I spent together before he died. I can still see his big, calloused hands as he made his way around that orange. I suppose every year since then I have repeated what I learned that day and every single time my mind goes back to him and the simple act that is now a special gift I will treasure for the rest of my life. The simple lesson was more than him teaching me how to peel an orange—he gave me a memory of my now long-gone father that I cherish each time I peel an orange.

The birth of the baby Jesus that we celebrate at Christmas was about as simple as could be. Born in a lowly stable and placed in an animal's manger. There was no great fanfare, no parades, no fireworks, and no breaking news reports. Even though prophets foretold his birth none of them were there awaiting his arrival. He quietly entered this world and, with the exception of some shepherds and eventually some wise men from a distant land, no one came to welcome him. Yet here we are, over two thousand years later, remembering his birth and celebrating Christmas. Even though his arrival was simple, he changed the world—one person at a time. Each Christmas, I remember my earthly father when I peel my oranges, and I remember the story of Jesus when I see those manger scenes.

Nothing is Everything

Vanessa Davis Griggs

"I hate Christmas, and I hate Santa Claus!"

I stopped pulling gifts out of a bag and turned to see who'd just spoken those words. A young girl with big brown eyes was looking at me. I turned my full attention to her. "Hi there. I'm Mrs. Goodwin."

"So, you're making sure we all have something for Christmas, huh?"

I smiled. "I'm merely one of Santa's helpers," I said.

"Sure," the young girl said. "Except I know the *real* truth. I may be ten, but everybody says I'm smart for my age."

"Ten, huh?"

"Yes, ma'am, going on eleven. That's my mother and little brother over there." She pointed. "Aaron's eight." Her braided hair had colored beads on the ends that swung in unison when she turned her head toward her family.

I nodded. "And what's your name?"

She grinned, exposing one missing bottom tooth and placed her hand on her hip. "Mariah."

"Mariah. That's a pretty name."

"Thank you. Not trying to be disrespectful, but you know I didn't name myself, right?" She smiled.

I nodded. "Indeed."

"Mariah, I hope you're not bothering this nice lady." Mariah's mother now stood before me.

I smiled. "Mariah's a dear-heart. We're merely having a cordial chat. I'm Victoria Goodwin."

Mariah's mother placed her hand over her heart. "Oh! Mrs. Goodwin, it's a pleasure to meet you. I'm Danielle Adams." She extended her hand. I did a fist bump instead. "Thank you for sponsoring this today. We truly do appreciate it. Truly."

"She's not wearing plastic gloves like the other folks here," Aaron said, noting my cloth white gloves. "Why do you wear those?"

"Because she's rich and she doesn't want germs and stuff getting on her hands," Mariah said, rolling her eyes. "Especially after what we've gone through with COVID. Wearing those is her way of protecting herself. Right, Mrs. Goodwin?"

"Mariah!" Danielle said, throwing a *mama-look* at her daughter that clearly stated, "*Cool it!*"

"Oh, she's fine." I turned to Mariah and Aaron. "Actually, I've worn gloves for decades. A little habit I picked up from my grandmother."

Mariah directed her eyes at my head. "Is that also why you wear a fancy hat?"

"It's huge, and the rhinestones are blinging!" Aaron said, stretching out his arm.

I smiled. "Actually, my grandmother wore hats to church. My grandmother was quite a classy woman. At least, I thought. Hats like these aren't as popular as they were back in the day. I wear mine now to honor those who came before me."

Danielle placed her hand on top of Aaron's head. "Again, Mrs. Goodwin, we thank you for this opportunity today. This is my first time needing to participate in something like this."

"And I *still* hate Christmas, and I *still* hate Santa Claus!" Mariah said.

"Mariah! Stop that! What have I told you?"

I nodded. "She's just expressing her true thoughts." I beckoned my assistant over. "Stacey, please take Mariah and Aaron to the gingerbread house kits."

"Yes, ma'am," Stacey said, smiling. "Come with me."

After they left, I turned to Danielle. "So, how are you, my dear?"

Danielle nodded. "I'm okay."

"No, I mean *really*. How are *you*?"

Tears began to form in her eyes. "It's been really tough. I've been trying, but it feels like every time I take one step forward, I get knocked two steps back. It's only me and my children. They're really both great children. I'm sure Mariah has you thinking differently but—"

"No. Mariah is fine. I like that she's not afraid to speak her mind. Don't stamp out her fire. I see a lot of myself in her."

Danielle wiped at her tears with her hand. I gave her a pack of tissue from my pocketbook. "Walk with me," I said in a desire to escape the earshot of others.

"I appreciate you taking the time to talk to me," she said. "I don't have family to turn to. You see, I grew up in foster care. The day after I turned eighteen and the money ended, they turned me out of their house. God knows I've made my share of bad decisions. But God also knows how hard I try to do all I can for my children." Danielle dabbed her eyes. "I love them so much; there's *nothing* I wouldn't do for them."

"I'd love for you and your children to come visit me at my house. I heard Mariah. I mean I actually *heard* her. I hear the hurt and disappointment she carries."

"I've tried to tell her we're still blessed in spite of everything. We have a roof over our heads and food on the table. But she sees others with nice things, and she doesn't understand why we're left to struggle. Christmastime is the hardest with all the other children talking about what they're getting or what Santa Claus actually brought them. It's just hard to explain the fairness of it all."

"I understand. That's why I want you to visit. I'd like to see if I can help."

"I don't want to impose. This event today is truly a blessing. I hate being a charity case, but I didn't have any other place to turn this year. It's been a rough." Danielle wiped more tears.

I placed my gloved-hand on her hand. "I get it. Believe me. So, when is a good day for you to visit?"

She chuckled. "Well, it's not like our calendar is booked. You tell me."

"Well, tomorrow is Sunday. We could attend church together and then go to my house for dinner, if that works for you."

Danielle smiled. "Yes. Tomorrow would be great!"

"Perfect," I said. "So, what type of things do Mariah and Aaron enjoy doing? What are their interests?"

"Well, Mariah is book smart, loves to read, loves using her hands, and all things technical. She enjoys creating and love, love, *loves* to draw," Danielle said. "Aaron enjoys helping me out in the kitchen."

"Mama, look what I got!" Aaron rushed over with a burst of energy. "We got to choose our own gingerbread houses! Mine is different. Ms. Stacey got this one special, just for me!"

"It's *especially* just for me, not special just for me." Mariah corrected him. She turned to Danielle. "I chose a traditional gingerbread house," she said.

"That's wonderful," Danielle said. "Guess what?"

"What?" Aaron said.

"Mrs. Goodwin has invited us to her house tomorrow." Danielle pressed her lips together. "She also invited us to go to church with her."

"Oh, great," Mariah said, obviously not thrilled. "Church."

"Mariah! Stop acting like we don't go to church!" Danielle said.

"I like going to church, Mama," Aaron said. "Those old ladies love giving me hard candy!"

Danielle's eyes grew wide. "Aaron, that's not nice."

"What? That they like to give me candy?"

"No. Calling them old ladies," Danielle said.

"But they *are* old. Sister Ross always says, 'I ain't no spring chicken!' You said that expression means she's old."

I turned to my assistant. "Stacey, please get Danielle's information." Then I turned back to Danielle. "My driver will pick you up tomorrow in time for church that starts promptly at 10:00 a.m."

Danielle smiled. "Thank you again, Mrs. Goodwin. We're excited!"

Sunday morning, I sat in my usual spot.

"Love that hat, Sister Virginia!" Hattie said. "Is it new?"

"No, it's one of my older hats."

"Well, you have so many. Your hat boxes must have their own room."

"Indeed," I said.

Hattie looked toward the entrance door. "Looks like a new crop of visitors today. All these folks showing up weeks before Christmas trying to get whatever handouts they can manage to wrangle." Hattie continued to look at the door. "They must have noticed your hat and decided to make you their mark for the day because they're headed our way."

"Hi, there!" a small voice said with excitement.

"Hi, there, Aaron!" I said with a smile. "Come and sit here," I said as I patted the spot next to my left side. Hattie now looked like she wanted to crawl under the pew. "Aaron, say hello to Sister Hattie."

"Hi, Sister Hattie!" Aaron said. "So where is your hat?"

"Excuse me?" Hattie said.

"Your name is Hattie so you should have a hat," Aaron said, grinning. "So, where's *your* hat?"

"I don't own one," Hattie said.

"You don't? Well, maybe Mrs. Goodwin will let you have one of hers. I'm sure she won't mind. She invited me, my sister, and my mother to church with her today. I love church!"

Danielle and Mariah walked up. "Aaron, I hope you're not bothering Mrs. Goodwin," Danielle said. "When he saw you, he took off running. I couldn't stop him."

"He's not a bother," I said. "Come sit with me. Mariah can sit on my other side here."

Mariah came and sat next to me. Danielle sat next to her.

Hattie stuttered. "You kids care for some candy? I have peppermint, butterscotch, and strawberry candy."

Aaron laughed. "Yes, please. Thank you."

I chuckled at our inside joke.

Pastor George Landris preached a sermon using different scriptural references. The first with Moses out of Exodus 4:2: "And the Lord said unto him, What is that in thine hand? And he said, A rod." The second with the prophet Elijah and a widow woman from 1 Kings 17:12: "And she said, As the Lord thy God liveth, I have not a cake, but a handful of meal in a barrel, and a little oil in a cruse: and behold, I am gathering two sticks, that I may go in and dress it for me and my son, that we may eat it, and die." The last one using Elisha and the widow's oil in 2 Kings 4:2: "And Elisha said unto her, What shall I do for thee? Tell me, what hast thou in the house? And she said, Thine handmaid hath not any thing in the house, save a pot of oil."

Pastor Landris' title was, "Nothing is Everything." He preached on how we may believe we have nothing, but when God is involved, *nothing* is *everything*. "God is asking you, 'What's in your hand?' Because our God, who stepped out on *nothing* and spoke what He desired to see, can use what you have and bless it exceedingly, abundantly, above all you can ask or think. We just have to trust Him and be obedient."

After leaving the House of the Lord, we went to my house.

"This is humongous!" Aaron said.

"Wow!" Mariah chimed in. "You're living large and in charge!"

"Oh, a house is just a house," I said. "It's true though: To whom much is given, much is required."

After we finished eating, I stood up. "I have something for all of you. Let's retire to the den."

"Whoa! Presents!" Aaron said, seeing the wrapped gifts in the den.

"Aaron, no one said these are ours," Mariah said.

I smiled. "But indeed, they all are."

Aaron jumped up and down. "Can we open them now? Please? I love presents!"

"Absolutely," I said. "Let's see what we have."

Mariah checked the tags. "There are three for me, three for Aaron, and one for you, Mama," Mariah said as she handed them out.

Aaron quickly ripped the wrapping off his first gift. He looked confused. "A mixer? Did somebody put my name on the wrong gift?"

"Oh, no. It's yours," I said.

"A mixer? I got a mixer?"

"Aaron!" Danielle's tone spoke volumes. "Tell Mrs. Goodwin thank you."

"Thank you," he whispered.

Mariah opened her first gift. "Wow," she said equally unenthused. "A drawing pad. Thanks."

Aaron opened his second gift. "Pans, baking utensils, and a decorating kit?"

I smiled. "Oh, those aren't just any pans; they're top of the line—used by top chefs."

Aaron glanced over at his mother, then back to me. "Thank you," he said, noting his mother's laser-focused, serious stare.

Mariah opened her second gift. "Colored pens and a complete paint set," she said, then looked at Danielle who was now staring hard at her. "Thanks, Mrs. Goodwin."

"You're so very welcome!" I said, knowing full well neither of them were excited about the gifts I'd chosen.

"Maybe I should save the last gift for when I get home," Aaron said, faking a smile.

"Oh, no. I want to see you open them," I said. "Go on; open the last one." I smiled.

Aaron looked at his mother who was pressing her lips tightly. He opened the last gift. "Gee, it's a cookbook."

"Not just *any* cookbook. That one is by a premiere chef," I said.

Danielle looked at the front of the book. "Hey, Aaron, we've seen him on television. This is Chef Kenan. He's *really* good and funny."

"Yeah," Aaron said. "He makes jokes while he's cooking."

Mariah opened her final gift. "Hey! It's that book I wanted! *Painting Perfection and Perfecting Your Craft: Your Gift Will Make Room For You.*" Mariah flipped through some of the pages. "I just saw her on television talking about this book. Thank you, Mrs. Goodwin. Wow!"

"Thanks so much, Mrs. Goodwin," Danielle said.

"Mama, you didn't open your present," Aaron said.

"Yes, Mama. You didn't open *your* gift." Mariah grinned.

"I was thinking about saving mine for Christmas," Danielle said.

"Oh, no. Open it now," I said.

Danielle opened her gift. "It's a camera and a printer! Thank you!"

Aaron walked over to his mother. "How come Mama got something nice and we got—"

"Aaron!" Danielle snapped before turning to me. "I am *so* sorry."

I held up my hand. "No need to apologize." I then turned to Mariah and Aaron. "Now, here's what I'd like. Take your gifts and use them to make a gift for each other."

"Excuse me?" Mariah said.

"Use what you've received here and make each other a gift for Christmas. In fact, make me a gift as well. Bring them here, and we'll exchange them on Christmas Eve."

"So, you want us to make each other and you a gift using what you gave us?" Mariah said.

"Yes."

"Mama too?" Aaron asked.

I smiled and looked at Danielle. "Yes, Mama too. Would Christmas Eve work for you?"

Danielle appeared to be taken aback. "You want us to come here Christmas Eve?"

"Only if you'd like to and don't already have plans that day."

"Oh, we don't have plans!" Aaron said. "And Mama's already said that Santa likely won't be stopping by our house this year. Not because I haven't been good...because I have."

"Aaron!" Danielle said. "What is wrong with you?"

"Mama loves calling my name!" Aaron said with a laugh. "As you say, Mama: The truth will make us free."

"You must need a family to spend Christmas Eve with," Mariah said with a smirk.

"Mariah Antoinette!" Danielle said, then turned to me. "Mrs. Goodwin, I don't know what has gotten into my children. I assure you they've been raised better than this. We will *definitely* have a conversation when we get home."

"They're fine. I don't mind hearing what they think. I'm a tough cookie; I can take it." I stood up. "I have truly enjoyed you all today. So, I'll see you on Christmas Eve."

They arrived Christmas Eve around two in the afternoon. Mariah didn't appear happy to be here.

"Is everything okay?" I asked Mariah after they put their gifts underneath the Christmas tree.

Mariah quickly glanced over at her mother. Danielle gave her *the look*. I was all too familiar with the "*You'd better not even!*" look.

"Yes, ma'am."

I nodded, knowing she'd likely been told to behave herself and not say or do anything to embarrass the family. "Great! Might I get you to help me with something upstairs?"

"I want to help, too!" Aaron said.

I weighed whether to let him come since my goal was to find out what was really going on with Mariah. I didn't want him to feel left out. "You know what, Aaron? Would you help Stacey finish setting the table in the dining room?"

Stacey looked at me knowing the table was already set. Realizing what I was doing, she smiled. "Yes, Aaron. I could use some help ensuring the table is ready."

Stacey and Aaron left, and Mariah and I went upstairs.

"Wow, this is beautiful," Mariah said when we entered my bedroom.

I motioned for her to sit on the couch. I cut to the chase not wanting to waste time playing games, "Okay, you're not where your mother can shut you down. Tell me what's going on with you."

Mariah appeared hesitant. I tilted my head to let her know it was okay to speak her mind. "I just think this is all dumb," she said.

I nodded. "Okay. Could you be more specific?"

"The gifts you gave us. I think they were lame. I mean, you're rich, and you gave me and my brother cooking and painting things. Then you tell us to make gifts for each other using those things. You could have given us better things like toys or computers or even one gaming system to share. My mama said we should be thankful because you didn't have to invite us over or give us anything. She always tells us that the world doesn't owe us anything. I get that. As I said the day we met: I hate Christmas, and a Santa Claus who gives to those who already have and little to nothing to those who have nothing. It's just not right!"

I nodded. "I hear you."

"You're rich, Mrs. Goodwin. You don't know what it's like to be us. This one room here is almost as large as our whole place."

"I'd like to show you something." I went and got a photo album and turned to a picture. "This is where and how I grew up." The photo was of a four-room house held up by stilt-stacked bricks. Three children stood together with chickens pecking at the ground. "This is me, my sister, and my baby brother."

"This was *your* house?" Mariah asked.

"Yes. As you can see, I haven't always been rich. So, I have *some* idea how you feel. In fact, I felt some of the same way about things as you when I was growing up. We would look forward to Santa Claus coming. On Christmas Day, my sister and I might get a doll, not even one our color. My brother would get a cheap plastic truck. We got a pair of socks, a few pieces of fruit, a few pieces of hard candy."

"Seriously?" Mariah asked. "That's it?"

"That was it. But there was lots of love in our home. So, when you think I don't know where you're coming from, you're wrong." The doorbell chimed. I smiled. "Looks like my other guest has arrived."

"You invited someone else?" Mariah asked.

"Yes. Remember, you said I needed a family to spend Christmas with." I laughed. "Looks like you hit *that* nail on the head."

"I wasn't trying to be rude or ugly saying that," Mariah said.

"It's fine. What did your brother say the other day? 'The truth will make us free.'"

We went back to the den. Both my guests were in there now. I hugged the woman there as I'd already hugged the man when he arrived earlier.

Mariah quickly covered her mouth in surprise. "You're her! You're the person on the book Mrs. Goodwin gave me!" She turned toward the man. "And you're the one on the book she gave Aaron! Look, Aaron!"

"Indeed, it's Chef Kenan in the house!" Chef Kenan smiled and fist bumped with Mariah and then Aaron.

"Hello, I'm Marcella." Marcella smiled and fist bumped like Chef Kenan had just done.

"It's really you! I love your paintings!" Mariah said. "I finished your whole book. I can't believe you're here! Wow! What an awesome surprise!"

"I'm happy to meet you," Marcella said. "Mrs. Goodwin has told me all about you."

"And Mrs. Goodwin asked me to prepare a meal for a king and some queens. I get to serve you all today with a few of my favorite recipes," Chef Kenan said. "*My* gift to all of you."

"I also brought your family a gift," Marcella said, looking at Danielle but handing it to Mariah.

Mariah took it, looked to her mother and then to me.

"You may open it," I said with a smile.

Mariah pulled off the Santa Claus wrapping. "Oh, wow! Look! It's a painting of us!"

Danielle placed her hand over her heart. "From the pictures I took with my camera." Looking at me, Danielle began to cry. "That's why you asked me to email pictures to you."

"Indeed," I said. "Painted and signed by a world-renowned artist." I winked at Marcella.

"That had to have cost you a lot of money!" Aaron said. "We look good!"

"And now for dinner," Chef Kenan said. "Let's eat while it's hot!"

It was one of the best meals I'd ever eaten by Chef Kenan.

"As my mother would have said were she alive today," I said, "Chef Kenan, you put your *foot* in that meal."

"Wait! What?" Aaron said, his eyes wide. "He put his foot in what we just got through eating?"

Marcella laughed. "I said the same thing when I first heard that expression. It's actually one of the highest compliments one can give a cook. It means it was awesome...that the cook stepped all up in it, figuratively speaking of course."

Aaron wiped his forehead. "Whew! That's a relief!"

We went back to the den. "Now it's time for the gifts you all brought," I said.

Mariah shook her head. "After this, I don't think we should ruin it with the things we made."

Chef Kenan patted his heart as he said, "Never downplay a gift from the heart."

"I concur," Marcella said.

"Agreed," I said. "So, let's see what awesome gifts we have here."

Aaron's gifts were cupcakes made "from scratch" using what I'd given him. Mariah painted her mother a beautiful house with the sun shining brightly on it and colorful flowers all around. She painted Aaron a star-filled night with a quarter-moon and a grinning Aaron riding the hook of the moon. My gift was a painting of me spinning in sunrays sporting a large hat and white gloves.

"Mariah, these are all so beautiful!" I couldn't help myself; I began to cry.

"Oh, it's nothing," Mariah said, shaking her head.

"No. These really *are* good," Marcella said. "Trust me, I've seen lots of paintings in my lifetime. You show great promise. Keep at it."

"Y'all are just being nice," Mariah said, lowering her head before looking back up. "Mrs. Goodwin, you have so much. This house. Money you can practically give away. Chef Kenan, you're famous. You've cooked for presidents. Ms. Marcella, you get lots of money from the sale of your paintings. Y'all can't possibly understand what it's like, these days anyway, seeing folks with *everything* when you have *nothing*."

I smiled, walked over, and pointed to a painting on the wall. "This picture here is one of my most prized possessions."

"I could have painted that one," Aaron said.

"True," Marcella said. "It's not that great if I have to say so myself."

"Right," Mariah said. "So, why hang that up when you have access to a great artist like Ms. Marcella and her paintings to choose from?"

I touched the painting. "When I was young, our family literally had *nothing* to give each other one year for Christmas. *Nothing*. So, my mother told us to *make* something to give to each other. She told us to use what we had in our hands which didn't make sense since we had nothing. My mother broke it down and said, 'Use your gifts and gift it to each other.'"

I paused, then continued. "So, my sister created a painting for each of us. Keep in mind, she didn't even have paint so she had to create colors from plants, food, and who knows what else."

"Wow!" Aaron said. "At least you gave me and Mariah something to work with to make our gifts."

I walked over and stood next to Chef Kenan and Marcella. "My brother loved hanging out with our mother who was quite the cook. She could literally take what seemed like *nothing* and make something wonderful out of it. So, for

Christmas, my brother baked each of us our own fancy dessert. It was famously good!"

"I get what you were doing, Mrs. Goodwin," Mariah said. "But who truly cares about what we just gave each other? Our classmates will be getting computers, televisions, clothes, and other things. We get to brag about giving each other homemade stuff." She smiled. "However, this year we can say we got to hang out with y'all."

"Well, I hope you take away that the best gift I ever received was from my mother who gave us love and encouragement and did all she could for us," I said.

"Just like our mother." Aaron smiled, ran over, and hugged his mother.

"Yes. Just like your mother," I said. "Also, understand that where you start is merely that: where you started. Material things are temporary: they break, go out of style, we outgrow them. But gifts from the heart, they're forever. I love Proverbs 18:16 that says, 'A man's gift maketh room for him, and bringeth him before great men.' That's true, is it not?" I looked at Marcella and Kenan and smiled.

Marcella laughed. "Well, it certainly turned out to be true for us. You see, what Mrs. Goodwin isn't telling you is how she was this great seamstress and clothing designer. For Christmas that year, she designed and sewed—without a bought pattern or a sewing machine—outfits for her sister, brother, and mother."

"Yes. And with her skill, dedication, and hard work, she became the mogul we all know and love today," Chef Kenan said. "The other part she failed to tell you is that I was that little brother who loved to cook."

Marcella smiled and dabbed her eyes. "And I am the sister who painted that painting on the wall." She pointed to the painting everyone just looked at.

"Wait a minute! What?" Mariah said. "Mrs. Goodwin, is your sister?"

"Yes. And she's a wonderful sister," Kenan said. "One who, to this day, inspires and blesses all whose lives she crosses and touches."

"Then my brother and I are just like y'all," Mariah said. "You started out with nothing, and now you have everything."

"I don't know about *everything*." I laughed. "Nevertheless, my gift to all of you was to show the truth: *Nothing is everything*," I said. "However, my most prized gifts have come from the heart. It's not about money; it's about cherished memories. If you learn to create memories, you'll *never* be without." I smiled, then hugged my sister, brother, and newly inspired family. "Merry Christmas."

Rock Quarry Christmas

Gus Guess

This is a fictionalized account of a true story because no one is still alive to be interviewed. The names are invented, the conversation loosely remembered, the opinions biased, even the number of participants is plus or minus five. But these things happened…

"1956 was a hard year," the old convict relayed to me over coffee and cards. "I'd gotten out of the Army after Korea and been on my way to the chain gang from the minute I walked away from the bus station in Atlanta."

Now we sat at a picnic table on the prison rec yard thirty odd years later. It was the morning of the prison Christmas program and we had come out early because Jimmy George wanted to pick a good place for the show.

The table he selected wasn't a surprise, it was the same one he always sat at any time he could make it to the yard. And it wouldn't have mattered if he had come last, this was his table. Everyone knew that. Prisoners respect the elderly. Especially the ones who had spent their lives inside, more because of their acts of defiance than their crimes committed.

"So leading up to Christmas that year we had been working six days a week in the rock quarry since before Thanksgiving. All the cons had been grumbling, but what can ya do?

The man, he has the gun and the sticks and the chow and the god-awful hole to use as punishment. We had nothing but tiny little knives we use to clip the ends off our cigars."

Some other men began to make their way to the yard now. Basketball games were always going on one side, volleyball in the pit the last warden had allowed to be made out of the sand left over from constructing the new prison was happening on the other. We would all be moving across the yard after the first of the year. This was still the same rec yard that cons had been walking around and relaxing on in the 1930s.

"We had worked the whole of Thanksgiving and eaten bologna sandwiches for lunch on hope. First I hoped we would only work 'til lunch, then that we would quit early in the afternoon. When the sun, at-dang-last, sat beyond those blue ridges to the west, there was still hope that supper would be special."

The prison staff was now beginning to show up on the yard. This and the Fourth of July program were the only times that everyone who could—did—turn out to see the shows put on by the inmates. All the suits and all the women who worked in the administration and medical areas came in groups of threes and fives. In summer, it was the softball games and footraces that drew the crowds. In winter, it is the display of performance talent, of which prison abounds, that brought out all the hidden people.

"Supper was soup of turkey scrap and chopped vegetables served with a slab of cold cornbread dressing and the last crumbs of the hope I'd begun the day with. We are too tired to protest. There is no way to drop a sledgehammer all day long and not be starved at the end of it. So, exhausted from the work and disappointment, I was glad for the soup I could just drink down and not have to chew."

Some of the most senior staff were just guards in '56. These aren't the ones who stood over the quarry and decided who got water and how much. Those men had died off years ago, as had most of the convicts they spit at from the lip of the walls. Hatefulness and hard labor rarely enhance a lifespan.

The Captain had been here as a fresh out of high school Army reject. Most of his relatives were generationally involved in the business of prisons, had raised families and drawn state pensions from careers in human misery. That lineage had kept him out of the hot sun and cold wind. He walked over to stand near the table and said, "Jimmy George, here for another Christmas I see. Going to do any dancing this year?" he asked with a chuckle before walking away without waiting on the "God-bless-you-n-yours" Jimmy George whistled through tightly held false teeth.

"It was bitter cold the whole week leading up to Christmas Day and my hands stung from the vibration through the ash wood handle of the sledge. These skinny things you see now trembling with old age were catcher's mitts then after two years of dropping hammers on rock. I had calluses so thick those days I'd crush cigars out in my palm and not feel the heat. But I felt the cold. It was just that though. A feeling. It didn't mean anything. My heart was as cold as my body and as unconcerned and as uncaring of what would become of the rest of my hopelessly abominable existence."

The chaplains' choir group began with a couple of hymns after the invocation, mostly as a nod to the reason for the season. Then followed Cowboy with a new stand-up comedy routine that he had worked up piece meal on all of us so that the whole was new and funny. The various bands that practiced a couple of hours a week in the gym with the chaplains' guitars and drum set each did two or three numbers of all the genres. Country, rap, blues, rock n' roll each had a turn and an audience. The program volunteers made their way among the staff and prisoners distributing sodas and small snack foods to any and all during the breaks between bands. These we ate and drank as Jimmy George returned to his interrupted tale of chain-gang Christmas past.

"I don't know who came up with the idea. It just sorta grew from 'we gotta do something' through the choices and repercussions of each until the merging of limits brought us all to agree on the hard logic of, 'Well, even if no one learns of our protest, the days of working in the quarry will be over with for all of us'. And so it was decided".

One of the men who worked in the quarry that day was so new to the job that he still swung his sledge in a full arc rather than the age old all-day-on-it method of just pick the thing up and drop it. He also still had a wife. The wife came for the New Year's Day visit allowed then and learned the story. She had a father who worked as a janitor at one of the newspapers in Atlanta or Lawrenceville. He told the story to a reporter there and in a few weeks the world learned.

"At lunch time on Christmas day while the guards warmed themselves by the fire barrel, forty of us sat down and laid aside our bologna sandwiches. We took out our cigar knives with the thin, razor sharp, two-inch blade and just above the lip of our brogan bootshoes, thirty-six of us pushed the blades through one leg each behind the Achilles' tendon and pulled."

"Some of the men yelled out from the pain. That got the attention of the guards but little else. What hands could be found toted the men up one by one out of the quarry and to the truck that ferried them back to the prison. By the time I was lifted from the cold ground, I'd had a long talk in the cool fresh air with the child born in Bethlehem so long ago. The Jesus that became a convict for a night and a day, who too had suffered so that others need not. I'd decided, 'This is the God I can relate to, believe in, have hope of, the One I'll serve.' Back in the prison we cons had our wounds cleaned, sewn shut, and bandaged. Then we returned to our racks assisted by grit or friends. No one, not warden or prisoner, gave a thought to the idea of a hospital and repairing the severed tendons."

Crippled for life and sentenced to life, Jimmy George, the last of the Buford Georgia Prison Rock Quarry survivors, got up with a tear in his age softened eye and clapped for the closing act of the day. With a distinctive slap-footed walk he made his way back to the infirmary that he had been allowed to leave to celebrate his final Christmas in the fresh open air.

Blessings in Disguise

Karen O. Allen

Joyful Christmas music on the radio, twinkling lights popping out around the neighborhood, homemade sugar cookies traced with colored icing, and eager retail stores with red and green merchandise. Shoppers dart from store to store, choirs rehearse for the upcoming Christmas cantata, bell ringers put the finishing touches on their carol arrangements, and the scent of pine and cinnamon is in the air. Decorations line the city streets, and the traffic gets heavier by the day. A sense of excitement pulses through my veins. The Christmas adrenaline rush is on.

Christmas is my favorite holiday. Always has been. Some of my earliest memories were when I lived on Greenwood Circle in Sylacauga, Alabama and all of the neighborhood kids would bring the adults together in the Jones' living room to watch a reenactment of the Christmas story. I was given the role of Mary one year, which I liked much better than being a wise man or the innkeeper.

Santa was also on my mind in these moments in the hopes I had been good enough for him to dole out a sampling of gifts with my name on them. The half-eaten cookie and empty glass of milk mesmerized me as a child, but the nibbled carrots lying on the outside step were all the proof I needed to know that Santa Claus and his eight flying reindeer had been at my house.

As a teenager, Christmas was centered around family, gift-giving, and church activities. When I became a newlywed, things changed. A lot. Christmas became more stressful with more demands pulling at my attention. What happened to the carefree days when Christmas was fun, more relaxed? The magic seemed to have gotten lost in the chaos of logistics and jobs.

I missed having my own Christmas tree in the corner of our downstairs family room. Parker bought one for me each year we dated. We enjoyed decorating it together. We decorated it the way I wanted to, of course. I missed Parker and I's dates driving around looking for Christmas lights in his red stick-shift Pinto with the customized Italian horn. I took great delight in seducing Parker whenever "Santa Baby" came on the radio. I missed our long talks on the front porch steps with the multi-colored Christmas lights strung in the prickly bushes behind us, providing a romantic ambiance to our conversations. When our late-night good-byes were reminiscent of the song "Baby, It's Cold Outside."

Now that we were married, we had other people to consider. We would have to share the holiday between his family and mine. Newlyweds do it all the time, right? But this newlywed had been uprooted two states away. Plus, my job in the hospital laboratory complicated things. Working as a medical technologist in a clinical laboratory is a twenty-four seven, 365-day-a-year career. People still get sick during the Christmas season. I didn't give as much consideration to that back in high school as I did when I entered the workforce.

How would Parker and I manage Christmas with my unyielding work schedule and a ten-hour drive back home? Our first Christmas wasn't supposed to be like this.

Luckily, I was able to manipulate a swap with a coworker. We had just enough time to drive home, say "Hello," exchange gifts, and get me back to work. We drove in late Christmas Eve and slipped into bed at my mother-in-law's house. No one stayed up to greet us. Parker's sister and her husband were asleep in the back bedroom having driven in from a few hours away.

The next morning, I noticed the table was set for eight. One for Mrs. Allen. Two for Cindy and Chuck. Three for the Sawyers, who were neighbors and close friends of the family. *Wait a minute. Why are there two more place settings? No, no, no! It can't be. Please don't be for us. Parker and I are supposed to go over to my parents' house for Christmas lunch. He must not have mentioned it to his mother. Why? Why would he not have said something? This is all wrong!*

Deciding that my mother would be more understanding than my mother-in-law, I mustered up the courage to call.

"Mother, I'm afraid that Parker and I are not going to be able to make it for lunch today."

My forced words were mixed with sobs to the point I could hardly catch my breath. My heart ached, and my emotions were strung out like a load of laundry hanging on a clothesline. With us not arriving until later, I knew my family would wait to open gifts from around the tree until we could get there. Although my parents only lived a few miles across town, it seemed like forever before we finally arrived. The conversation between Parker and I was stifled during the drive other than to make a firm decision to rotate Christmas Day lunch between his family and mine. Housing accommodations would be likewise. That was the fair thing to do for all concerned.

The next Christmas was harried with less time to visit. Our limited time prevented us from being *anywhere* and seeing *anyone* for long enough. We adhered to the pre-established plan to spend most of our time at my parents' house that year. While visiting my mother-in-law, however, an unsettling argument arose. Tears flowed, voices raised, and tensions heightened. Nobody was happy and that certainly included me.

Christmas Day came and went before it was time to be on the road again. As usual, I had to be back at work the next day. I knew we would be very late getting home, but I convinced Parker I could sleep on the drive back.

We left later than planned. Our orange Datsun was jam-packed with Christmas presents, luggage, pillows, and the dog. We tied a few things onto the luggage rack to leave space in the back seat for my sister. Nancy decided at the last minute to go with us to spend part of her Christmas break in Cajun country. A new environment from the first grade class, she thought, might be a welcome change.

We were only five hours into our ten-hour drive home when we started looking for a place to eat and purchase gas. Since it was still Christmas Day, our choices were almost non-existent. We would have to settle for the first thing we could find.

Parker decided to get off the interstate in hopes that our options would be better. He drove into the city to survey for open restaurants and gas stations. The gas gauge was on "E" and dropping fast. Desperation set in.

Ah-ha! There's one! Finally. Much relieved, Parker pulled into the station. Lights were on inside the building and another car was at the pump. He filled the tank and got back in the car.

"Now to find food," he said.

We gazed across the dark streets looking for a business with their lights on. Anything would do. Just something to put food into our growling bellies. The turkey and dressing from lunch was long gone, and we had not thought to pack a sandwich in our haste to leave.

Parker decided to head the other direction for a more comprehensive look. As he turned left onto a side street, we were jolted by a sudden crash in the rear of the car. Our Datsun spun around a few times throwing us back and forth before finally coming to a stop. We were stunned speechless. Nancy broke the silence from the back seat.

"There's fire back here!" Her voice was shaken.

I turned around to look from the front seeing a flash of orange-yellow light. The fire was behind the back seat close to the rear wagon where everything was packed. The three of us reacted without hesitation. Nancy opened the back door and ran one direction. Parker opened the driver's door and ran out the other side. I opened the passenger door and grabbed Rosceaux who grunted at my grasp which was swift and firm. I was the last one out of the car. I ran as fast as I could while struggling to hold the dog. My momentum didn't take me far before I fell into the grass on top of Rosceaux. He grunted harder in pain, and I let out a muffled scream having my breath knocked out of me.

Gathering to my feet, I realized I had left my purse behind. *Oh no! My driver's license, wallet, money, keys, credit card. Too late now.* I pushed those disturbing thoughts aside. *At least I saved the dog.* But where were Parker and Nancy? No sooner had the thought entered my mind when Nancy came walking up beside me putting her arm around me. Parker soon joined us. We looked at each other and hugged. Tears welled up in my eyes.

"Here, use this as a leash for Rosceaux." Parker unbuckled his belt and handed it to me. "Let me take him."

I was still holding him, but his forty-pound body was getting heavier by the minute. I wondered why Parker had not grabbed Rosceaux before darting out of the car, but didn't ask.

You can never be sure how you will react in an emergency situation until it happens. Will you panic? Will you freeze? Will you kick into gear? Somehow, I reacted with a sense of peace and calm. I admit it felt like I was in a dream, but it was far, far from a dream.

Within seconds following the crash, the car was engulfed in flames. Our hasty escape was none too soon. I was perplexed as to how it all had happened. And how fast it happened.

I could see another car beyond the flames. I assumed it was the vehicle that had struck us. Parker admitted he must have turned in front of the oncoming car though he never saw it approaching. I didn't either. It seemed to have come out of nowhere.

Christmas presents were strewn all over the road. The hatch had flown open tossing our new prized possessions onto the pavement as the car spun round and round. Gifts from the top of the car were also splattered on the road.

I stood there numb and in disbelief gazing at our car in flames. Sirens could be heard from the approaching fire engine and police car. A local news channel van was not far behind. There was no need to hurry. It was too late. The car that my Daddy had bought me for college had served its purpose well. Now it was gone. So was my purse with everything in it. The Christmas gifts inside the car. Gone. The beautiful hand-stitched bell pull made by my mother-in-law. Gone. My new light blue, puffy, calf-length coat from Mother and Daddy. Gone. Parker's camera. Gone. So many things. All gone. I reminded myself they were just material things. The important thing was that we were safe and unharmed. All three of us. No, four.

As the flames grew higher and hotter, I watched with thankful eyes. A quiet prayer floated into my thoughts as I thanked the Lord for keeping us safe. There was glory in that prayer, praise to the Almighty who rescued us from the fiery flames. He pushed us into safety with His caring and protective hand.

A fleeting thought also passed through my mind about those destined to a fiery hell. Why would anyone choose such a fateful end when they did not have to?

We watched the firemen put out the flames leaving a black shell of a car. We had been hit directly on the gas tank. The fireman told us had we not filled our car with gas moments earlier, it would have exploded upon impact from the fumes. Instead of exploding, however, it just burned.

Material possessions can be replaced. Sure, it would cost money, but insurance would cover much of it. A tremendous amount of work would be required to report every item lost, but at least we were alive to do it.

We gathered our salvageable belongings from the street. Our open suitcases were in the street. Most of the gifts that had been tied to the top of the car were saved. We had never used the luggage rack before.

The police drove us to a nearby hotel. We slept very little and arose early the next morning. Parker arranged for a rental car to drive home. I called my workplace. This was a Christmas I might have forgottenut now that would never be possible.

The next Christmas I refused to go home, not wanting to risk the trauma we had experienced the year before. Another car fire was unlikely, but I couldn't stand the thought of all the stress and tears. No, we would stay in Louisiana and enjoy Christmas at home around our own Christmas tree. Just Parker, me, and Rosceaux. We did. And it was absolutely awful! I cried. But they were homesick tears. I promised myself I would never, ever do that again. Even with the hassles and the chaos, not being surrounded by family on Christmas Day was unbearable. I rediscovered the blessing of family as being one of my most meaningful gifts.

Fortunately, we didn't have to make any decisions the next year because Parker was transferred back to Alabama. We would not have to spend more than an hour on the road coming and going from our house to Sylacauga. There would be no decision as to which bed to sleep in. We still adhered to the rotation plan about where to eat Christmas lunch. Overall though, Christmas Day was much easier and more enjoyable. Rosco (we changed from the Cajun spelling) could be left at home. Those difficult years were behind us. Or were they?

For the next two years, Parker and I had a car accident during the Christmas season. My car was totaled on the way to work early one morning when a sleepy driver hit a bridge, flipped his car, and landed right in front of mine. I was thankful to have slowed down when his weaving raised my suspicions. Otherwise, his car would have landed on top of mine. The next year Parker's truck was rear-ended. At least it was fixable and not totaled. Neither of us were injured—hallelujah!

Needless to say, the month of December made us both leery of sitting in the driver's seat even with a fire extinguisher under it. In fact, every car we own now has a fire extinguisher.

Parker and I have lived in Birmingham, Alabama for more than thirty-five years now. For the last two decades of my career, I worked in a research lab or office that closed on Christmas Day with a few extra days added on. That simplified matters tremendously.

I have since retired from working in health care and now serve as organist for my church. Of course, playing an organ requires weekend and holiday work . . . especially during the Christmas season. Here we go again!

A Homeless Christmas

W. R. Benton

The old looking man shivered and dropped another piece of wood into the hungry flames in the interior of a steel fifty-five-gallon drum. He was cold and all he'd had for supper was a quart of malt liquor beer and now he needed food or more drink, except he had no money for either. While he was forty, he looked and felt sixty-five or seventy most of the time, or so he thought at the odd times he shaved. Being homeless had aged him and a glance in a mirror always proved that point. Times had turned rough, and this was the best he could do now. Each time he took a breath, he could see a white puff of air, like he was smoking. It was cold, but this would be the warmest he'd be all night, unless something changed. The shelters were all full, so it was time to root hog or die.

"Spider, how long have you been on the streets, man?" Crow asked. None of the men they knew used their real names, only nicknames. Most used a moniker they'd had in the service.

"Forever and a day," Spider replied. "How about you?"

They were thin men, near six feet tall, malnourished, and neither had had a bath, haircut, or shave in over a year.

Both men often drank too much, but neither touched drugs. Crow, a Black man, often said, "We can get a quart of whiskey for the price of two little pain pills, and I need a drink. I come back to the world after the war in Iraq and found I no longer fit in. I was way different than the people walking around then. I was angry and would fight at the drop of a hat, but I had to watch myself because in a fight, I fought to kill, not win a fight."

"I returned from Nam a basket case, really messed up inside, but nobody cared. I tried to get help from the VA, and they put me on a waiting list in 1968, but I've never heard from them since. My old lady left me, mainly because I'd sit up all night drinking and holding a loaded shotgun in my hands. I kept the house dark once the sun went down, knowing the VC couldn't see well in the dark. Then I lost my job for coming to work drunk and threatening to kill my boss. It was shortly after that my only child died of crib death. From that point, well, my productive life was over, and here I am. I didn't care if I lived or died. I still ain't sure why I didn't die back in 1969 in the jungles of Nam, man."

"My story is pretty much the same, except after I had a few drinks I liked to fight, like I said a few minutes ago, and that landed me in jail more than a few times. I drank up the rent money my old lady had set aside, and here I am. I could have stayed with family, but they don't drink. I have to drink, just so I can sleep at night, without the dreams. I may have left Iraq, but the war never left me."

Out of the blue, Crow said, "Merry Christmas, brother."

"Is it that time of year again, my man?"

"Uh-huh. I hate the season too."

"Why? It's the birthday of Jesus."

Crow's eyes narrowed, his tone was cold and flat when he said, "I don't want to talk about it right now, okay?"

"Sure. Let's get back to how we became homeless. Why'd you drink? I had bad dreams with death, dying, and lots of crimson blood. I drank to be able to sleep." Spider said and then thought, *I must have been in a bloody firefight or battle around Christmastime some year in Nam. Only I can't remember every battle I was in during my three tours. I don't think so good these days and I don't know if it's because I'm old or drinkin' too much. Seems my memory works, but only at times and never when I need it to work.*

"If I didn't drink, I couldn't sleep at night either," Crow said. He shivered and added, "Colder than a banker's heart out here this evening. We'll be up all night feeding this fire."

A sudden, hard gust of wind blew some of the dry snow on the ground around the two men. As the snow moved, it looked like little white dust devils moving in the wind. "Must be well below zero out here right now."

"It's cold, but we've both seen it colder. Crow, after all we have done for America, does it anger you that they don't give a care about us? The VA takes our names, but that's as far as they go. Heck, I've heard of men dying for the want of care in their waiting rooms."

"Yeah, it pisses me off at times. We killed America's enemies and were almost killed, more than once, for this nation. Some of us gave up our sanity to protect America. I have a partial steel skull, was shot in both legs, and my hearing is all but gone. I took the head wound one night in the bush when Al-Qaeda overran our company. Out of 85 men, a dozen of us survived. I . . ."

Crow's voice dropped to the point he could not be heard. When Spider looked at him, he was staring straight ahead, with tears running down his thin ebony cheeks. His body shook as he gave a loud sigh.

"You're okay, man. We're back in the world. That battle happened close to Christmas, didn't it?"

"Uh-huh, Christmas Eve as a matter of fact."

"I fought a battle on Christmas day, 1969. All of us that survived were badly wounded. I get depressed every holiday season because I can't put the battle behind me. It's been years and I'm still in Nam each Christmas."

"I never left Iraq, and it's in me every single day. I've considered suicide so many times, but I lack the guts to kill myself."

"Sometimes I wonder why God let me live when better men than me died. Sometimes late at night I relive a deadly battle I had in Iraq. I can vividly hear the screams of the wounded and the cries of the dying. I can remember the coppery smell of blood, stench of human waste, the urine having a strong ammonia scent, and strong smell of cordite in the air. Sometimes, not very often now, but I wish I'd died that day. W . . . why did I live . . . when so many others . . . died?" Spider gave a loud moan, shook, and began crying. His body quivered violently as he cried, unashamed.

Crow gave him time to release his emotions, then moved to his friend's side and said, "Let it out, man. I've been there. I have a story like yours, just a different war. My dreams still bother me, just like yours do you, man."

"Nobody gives a care about us, except other veterans!" Crow said, his tone filled with anger. "And most of the people living in the streets like animals are veterans! If people honestly cared, they'd help us. Just like in Nam or Iraq, man. We're . . . we're . . . alone and nobody gives a care about us. They used us and then tossed us to the side because we ain't nothin' no more."

"Chill, my man, because it don't mean nothin'."

"Would you be embarrassed to, uh, pray with me? If you don't want to, that's okay."

"You believe in God?" Spider asked as he watched his friend wipe his eyes with the backs of his soiled hands. His tone was soft.

"Yes, I believe in God, don't you?"

"We're back on speaking terms now, but for years I was angry at Him. I'll pray with you, but I have to warn you, I don't do the job very good."

"Just pray. It always lightens my heart." Crow removed his hat and lowered his head. Spider placed his arm around his best friend's neck and thought of a prayer.

Then Spider lowered his head and said, "Lord, we ain't much. Don't have two nickels to rub together, and we don't go to church regular, but You know me from my other prayers. My friend and I need You to help us get through the holidays. Now, I know Christmas is your birthday, which is important, but we have other memories that are stronger than your birth. Memories of good men dying and being maimed in a bad war. Send us love and put joy in our hearts as the world celebrates your birth, Jesus. Show us a sign this Christmas will be different. This I ask in the name of Jesus. Amen."

Suddenly Crow said, "Look at the sky! Do you see it?" He was pointing at the black western horizon.

A falling star with a long, burning tail was seen in the cold night air.

"God heard your prayer. Surely that's a sign that he heard you."

Spider grinned and said, "Here come the police and I hope they're not here to harass us and make life hard. Not cold enough for me to want to go to jail yet, that's another month off."

"They look to be carrying blankets and small bags. Maybe this Christmas will be better than the others. I hope they have some food."

"They have food, I can smell it."

"Merry Christmas, my man," Crow said, his face reflecting his joy. Just the thought of warm blankets and maybe some hot food made him happy.

"Merry Christmas, my friend and may a God give us many more."

"Merry Christmas," the police officers said as they neared the two homeless men.

Looking up, Crow saw another falling star and smiled as he said, "Merry Christmas to all of you officers and may God bless each of you."

The story is my attempt to see our holidays in the eyes of a homeless veteran. Remember them this season, as well as year-round, and consider donating to a shelter to help feed and clothe them. Many of them are veterans of various wars and conflicts, and we owe them more than we can ever pay. Giving is much better than receiving, so bring a little joy to our homeless. If you lack money, prayers are free and more important. If possible, help with both money and prayers. I pray the Good Lord will bless you and yours during the Christmas season.

Halfway to Nashville

Jennifer Horne

She is driving north on Highway 65, still in Alabama but getting close to the Tennessee border. It is a relief to be in hill country again after the claustrophobia of Black Belt pine forests, broken only by the occasional catfish farming operation.

She passes a large green sign, welcome shimmer in the dark night, and admires the simplicity of its message: town names followed by miles. No equivocation.

Halfway to Nashville, then, she thinks. Also, halfway from home.

The words echo in her brain, *halfway to Nashville, halfway from home,* like a song she heard once and can't quite remember.

Halfway to Nashville,
halfway from home.
What would come next?
Halfway to leaving you,
and halfway on my own.
Not a bad slant rhyme, home/own.
She hums to herself,
Well, I'm halfway to Nashville,
halfway from home,
halfway to leaving you and
halfway on my own.

She is, she admits, not leaving anyone. Not for long, anyway. She is headed to Nashville on this Friday night in December to stay at the conference center near Vanderbilt where she and her husband, Brentley, had gone for a marriage enrichment retreat last spring, when the trees were greening and the air was warming and she had felt hopeful that they too could find the sap rising again.

She has been dreaming of babies. Plump, soft, cuddly, sweet-smelling babies. The twins, born when she was twenty-two and she and Brentley had just finished college, are now in college themselves. She figures she has a few more good eggs left, but when she brought it up with Brentley in September, right after the girls went back to school, he just looked at her as though her head was on fire. Shortly after that he went for a long, long run.

She only plans to stay one night. Or possibly two. The tree is decorated, the presents are wrapped, she's attended all the parties she was invited to, and the twins are off on a ski vacation and won't be home for a few days yet.

But suppose she weren't? Suppose she were leaving for good. What would she have taken with her? She had stopped at the ATM while leaving town, for a little extra emergency cash.

I've got . . . one hundred dollars and

two cans of beer.

Does that imply that she would drink and drive? It doesn't have to say that she is drinking the beers, just that she has them.

What if it were sort of a countdown, three two one?

I've got

three hundred dollars,
two cans of beer.
—she has just filled up at the last exit, so
one full tank
–another slant rhyme coming
and I won't look back
–the beer rhyme is easy
'til I'm far away from here.
–maybe too easy.
'til I'm far away from fear.

She is not afraid of Brentley. He is completely civilized. But if a woman were leaving her husband, or lover, and was afraid, what would come next? By now she is driving through the night heedless of mileage, sipping on coffee she brought in a travel mug and wondering whether she might start up a new career as a Nashville songwriter: "Hey everybody, let's give a hand to Brantley McGehee!" (In her fantasy she has taken her maiden name back, although she had been mildly bothered by it ever since Debbie Carl in fifth grade would tease her by calling her McGee-Hee-Haw. Maybe she could change it to McGee, with an echo of "me and Bobby.")

She is Brantley and he is Brentley. Brentley Spencer. When Brentley moved from Virginia to her high school in senior year, the homeroom teacher had such a strong accent that when she said "Brentley" it might as well have been "Brantley" and they both answered "Here!" in their young, clear voices, and that is how they met cute.

Brantley's fire, Brentley's warmth. Brantley's spark, Brentley's glow. It had worked for them for a long time.

Brentley is named after his family's former plantation in Virginia, which was named after a stream in England near where his ancestors had their home, which the family would like you to think was a baronial mansion. Brantley is named after the song "Brandy," which her father was besotted with when she was born. She is not actually named Brandy because her mother put her foot down and insisted on a name with a little more dignity. She allows herself to be called "Bran" by her family and friends, but only her father gets to, occasionally and with affection, call her Brandy.

Brentley has no nicknames. Not Brent, not Lee, certainly not The Brenster, Brentano, Bentley, or Spence. Always just Brentley.

Not that she would tell him, but her Baptist-upright father would not want to know that the thought of leaving Brentley had ever even crossed her mind. Only the worst kind of abuse or adultery would warrant that.

And if that?

I've been

too tired to fight you,

too scared to leave,

but I've packed my bags

and I'm making tracks

—it would be neat to speed up the tempo here

and it's not you I grieve.

—no

and it's the waste of time I grieve.

She likes the bounce of it but then she sings the "halfway to Nashville" chorus part and realizes that she's used "leave" twice. Too repetitious.

I've been

too tired to fight you,

too scared to . . . go,

but I've packed my bags

and I'm making tracks

—what rhymes with "go"? No, row, so . . . or if she goes a little country, "more."

and I'll never see you no more.

—or

and you'll never see me no more.

—yes, that's better. More assertive.

Of course Brantley does not use double negatives. But neither does she drink cans of beer, nor is she fleeing an abusive man.

She is well beyond halfway to Nashville now, in fact probably three-quarters of the way.

Things need to take a turn toward the positive, she thinks.

What comes after leaving? Finding, perhaps.

I'll find

something to live for.

—yes

Someone to be.

—what if she did take McGehee back, leaving Brantley Spencer behind?

I can change my name,

get beyond the pain

—what pain? The pain the imaginary *he* gave the imaginary *her.*

you took pleasure in inflicting on me.

—no. "In inflicting" would not do. It was too hard to say, especially combined with "you took," like a tongue-twister. And the "you" needed to be more like a "ya."

ya took pleasure in puttin' on me.

She sang back to herself what she had so far, adding in some throaty umhmms after each verse. It reminded her a little bit of the umhmms in the song "Mr. Frog Went a Courtin'" that her mother used to sing her to sleep with as a child: "Mr. Frog went a courtin' he did ride, umhmm, umhmm. Mr. Frog went a courtin' he did ride, umhmm, umhmm. Mr. Frog went a courtin' he did ride, sword and a pistol by his side, Mr. Frog went a courtin' he did ride, umhmm." She had fought going to sleep so as to hear the story of Mr. Frog courting Miss Mousie and their subsequent wedding, but try as she might she never made it past the earliest wedding guests. What happened at the end?

An English professor in college had told her that the song went back to Elizabethan times and was a veiled treatment of possible French suitors to Queen Elizabeth.

She wasn't sure if she believed that. And of course Queen Elizabeth had never married.

What did she believe?

I *believe in*

a future that's . . .

better than this.

—she did.

And I promise myself . . .

And I swear to myself

that I'll never again

—well, this was a love song of a sort, wasn't it? A breakup song?

be captivated by your kiss.

—no

captured by your kiss.

Umhmm. Umhmm. Umhmm.

While putting a stack of clean, fluffy towels in Brentley's bathroom last week she had found a book in the cabinet under the sink. Not a *Penthouse* or a *Playboy* or even his *Times* crossword puzzles, but a book titled *Always a Woman.* She looked at the back cover. "A woman has needs," it said. *Dang straight*, she thought. "Even if she takes on the roles of mother, chauffeur, cook, household organizer, and bookkeeper, she is still a woman. Is your wife feeling neglected? Has she been pulling away emotionally or physically?" Had she? "Find out how God intends for a man and a woman to have a loving, close relationship in the context of marriage." God in the bedroom? No thank you. "Men, don't take your wives for granted." Did he? "Here for the first time are the techniques and secrets of a marriage counselor with thirty years' experience and a proven record of helping men learn how to keep the woman in their life not only their best friend but their lover, companion, and soul mate."

This did not sound like Brentley at all, but no one else could have put it there. Had he meant for her to see it? Marriage could be the biggest puzzle of all…what got said, what didn't.

She had wondered idly whether the title *Always a Woman* had been taken from the Billy Joel song. Quoting from songs could be tricky; usage fees were prohibitively expensive. As permissions editor at a small publishing house specializing in outdoors and cooking titles, she had had to nix

"Strawberry Fields Forever" as a recipe name, concerned that the full weight of the Beatles music licensing legal team might fall on little In & Out Books.

She was still holding the book in her hand, she had realized, and so she had placed it back under the towels. Food for thought.

Two days ago she had asked him again whether he wouldn't like to try for another child.

"No!" he had said. "No, I wouldn't! Bran, we'd be sixty when we finished raising him. Or her."

"Sixty's the new fifty," she'd said, trying to lighten the tone of things.

He got that exasperated look, the one that said "You're trying to use your womanly skills to dance around the subject." He sighed. "You don't fix empty nest syndrome by finding another egg to hatch. The point is to find your new thing, or spend more quality time with your soul mate."

Ah, she'd thought. *The book.* She said, "But *why* can't we just have another baby? We were always good at that."

He smiled. "We were." Then he came across the room and hugged her. "But we're in a different place now. We just are."

Why did things have to change? What was wrong with wanting things to stay the same? And why did her brain generate so many questions and so few answers?

She loved the smell of babies, the feel of them in her arms. With Christmas coming on, she was thinking of baby Jesus, and how Mary must have held and nursed and cuddled him. Oh dear. This was five different kinds of wrong, being envious of the mother of Jesus because she had a new-born. In some accounts, Jesus had brothers, and maybe even sisters. Maybe it wasn't too late for her to have another child. Or two.

Brantley drove along, mind wandering, tires humming on the pavement as she hummed her song, remembering a book on songwriting she'd worked on a few years back. Something about a bridge, to break up the repetition of the stanzas, the way the bridge she was crossing now broke the monotony of the freeway. Similar but different. For some reason this part came easily, once she figured out she wanted to end with "gone." After a few tries she had:

Too many times I looked the other way,
Too many nights I was your pawn,
Too many times I let you make me stay,
But now my stayin' days are gone!

She sang it through once or twice to be sure she had it, rising in volume at the end. Who doesn't like singing loudly and alone in the car, voice filling the space like air fills a balloon?

Though it was only late afternoon, it was now fully dark, and she considered just turning around at the next exit and going home. But Brentley was at the hunting lodge with his doctor friends (though he did not hunt), and she didn't want to kick around the house alone all weekend, and she didn't quite feel like calling a girlfriend, and besides she needed to be in some kind of motion.

Recently the house had been having a series of small plagues. One morning they woke up and went into the kitchen, and the counters were covered in little black ants. She sprayed and wiped them off the counters by the hundreds—

they didn't bite—and the next day they were gone. Then two days after that she had walked into her bathroom and her house slippers had made crunching sounds, as though cereal were spread across the floor, but instead there were a dozen or so small snail shells scattered on the tiles.

The night before, long-legged crickets had shown up in the garage, not the cute brown Jiminy Cricket types, but gangly, gray-brown-speckled insects who hopped disconsolately around the stained cement floor.

What had the plagues been for in the Bible? A punishment?

Had she done something wrong?

She was almost to Nashville.

She sang the song all the way through, loud, like she meant it, like she had lived it:

Well, I'm halfway to Nashville,
halfway from home.
Halfway to leavin' you
and halfway on my own.
I've got
three hundred dollars,
two cans of beer,
one full tank
and I won't look back
til I'm far away from fear.
Umhmm. Umhmm.

Yes, I'm halfway to Nashville,
halfway from home.
Halfway to leavin' you

and halfway on my own.
I've been
too tired to fight you,
too scared to go,
but I've packed my bags
and I'm making tracks
and you'll never see me no more.
Umhmm. Umhmm.

Oh, I'm halfway to Nashville,
halfway from home.
Halfway to leavin' you
and halfway on my own.
I'll find
something to live for,
someone to be,
I can change my name,
get beyond the pain
ya took pleasure in puttin' on me.
Umhmm. Umhmm.

Too many times I looked the other way,
Too many nights I was your pawn,
Too many times I let you make me stay,
But now my stayin' days are gone!

Oh, I'm halfway to Nashville,
halfway from home.
Halfway to leavin' you
and halfway on my own.

I be-
lieve in
a future that's
better than this,
and I swear to myself
that I'll never again
be captured by your kiss.
Umhmm. Umhmm.
Umhmmmm.

Instead of going straight to the conference center, she would drive down Music Row. As Brantley McGee. She was far from tired, and it might be nice to see some other humans before she sequestered herself for the night.

In town, she headed over the viaduct and into downtown. She rolled the windows down, letting in the crisp, cold air. Approaching Music Row she could feel the energy, as though a dial had been turned up, and suddenly she was in it: a full-on sensory blast with bright lights flashing and zig-zagging in all colors, country music pouring out of the doors, people filling the sidewalks and cars filling the streets like the State Fair midway and the high school football game and Times Square all rolled into one.

"Whoo!" whooped Brantley McGee. "Hot dang!"

As she yelled, she caught the eye of a slightly pudgy teenage boy in boots, jeans, chambray shirt buttoned up to the neck, and tan felt cowboy hat. He looked back at her, reached to the rim of his hat, and tipped it, with chivalric politeness, then turned the corner.

Brantley smiled to herself, a little embarrassed, a little touched.

Maybe she'd park, look for the art gallery she'd visited last spring. She remembered which block, so she found a spot, stepped into the December evening, and began walking. Plenty of people, plenty of lights—she felt safe enough. After circling the block twice, sure she was in the right place but unable to find the gallery, she decided to ask. She stepped into a decent-looking place where three Santas, in full Santa get-up but wearing cowboy boots, were drinking at the bar, boot heels hooked on bar stools.

"Um…excuse me?"

The Santas turned in unison.

"I'm looking for the art gallery that I think used to be on this block last year?"

"Gone," said the first Santa.

"Out of business," said the second.

"Tattoo place now," said the third.

A very pregnant waitress came out from the kitchen, door swinging behind her.

"Ma'am?"

"Aren't you a bit far along to still be working?" popped out of Brantley's mouth.

"Aren't you a little rude to be asking?"

One of the Santas snorted.

Brantley apologized, profusely, excessively. To compensate, she ordered a round for the Santas and left an excessively large tip, then beat it back to her car and drove to the conference center.

The nice young man who checked her in told her that he had put her in a room with no one adjoining, so she could lock the shared bathroom door and have it to herself. "We try to do that for any women here on their own," he said, glancing for a flickering instant at her wedding ring.

In her little nun's cell of a room, sitting up reading in the single bed, she felt calm. Nothing else need be done or decided for the moment. She was in a parenthetical space, a pause in the main narrative. Not so much in retreat as briefly hiding from reality.

But what if she didn't, or couldn't, get pregnant again? She pondered other careers, beyond becoming a writer of country music hits. Last week they had entertained clients of Brentley's at a very upscale, hip restaurant whose chef had done a book with In & Out. On the appetizer menu was something called "Forager's Finds," with wild mushrooms, watercress, persimmons, pecan-flour crackers, and a tiny cup of dandelion wine. The idea of supplying a restaurant with foraged foods, spending her days walking through the woods looking for edibles, appealed to her. Brantley did not currently, however, know the difference between a pansy and a . . . what? A petunia. There would be a slight learning curve.

She had, she remembered, enjoyed working on a book titled *The Redneck Vegetarian,* a humorous but innovative cookbook that took as its epigraph the phrase "No dang tofu." There were chapters on "Life without Fatback," "Fruit: Your New Friend," "Cornbread, I Sed," "Why I Fry," and "What to Eat at Granny's Sunday Chicken Dinner." Her favorite chapter was "Thank God Beer and Whiskey Aren't Made with Meat." She had suggested a list of exceptions as an Afterword, including accepting something that someone has caught or shot and brings to you as a gift ("Beware of

Greeks Bearing Meats"), and the author had been happy to incorporate her ideas.

Her phone rang. Brentley. Which was surprising, as the lodge was out of the reach of any cell towers, by design. One of the doctors who owned it was known for saying, after a couple of bourbons, "Any woman who needs to find us"—and here he would smirk—"*for whatever reason,* is just going to have to come to us."

She picked up. "Where are you? Aren't you at the lodge?"

"Where are you?"

"Nashville. The retreat center. I left you a note."

"Those guys are idiots. I'm home."

"I thought I'd see that quilt exhibit at the Frist. You know, I missed it in Montgomery." For some reason, although she was not dyslexic in other ways, her brain always rescrambled the letters to make it the First Museum. Like when she once misread a bumper sticker that said "I <3 My Saturn" as "I <3 May Sarton."

But there her mind had gone, off pondering misreadings, and Brentley was talking. "Come back. I miss you," he said.

"I will. After the museum in the morning. I'll see you tomorrow." She hung up.

And she would come back, she decided. Christmas was coming, the girls would be home with stories of school and friends and adventures, and she would hug them and baby them and enjoy their time together. Whatever this was about, she was realizing, it wasn't really about Brentley after all. Knowing that, she was already halfway home.

Did you enjoy reading the first edition of *Gritty Southern Christmas Anthology?* If so, please leave an honest review wherever you interact: Amazon.com, Goodreads, or any of your social media platforms.

Meet the Authors

ANN H. NUNNALLY is a retired minister, author, and conference speaker. She is the creator and CEO of "An Encouraging Word with Ann Nunnally," a nonprofit, tax-exempt organization established to minister to the body of Christ worldwide through conferences, evangelical outreaches, and writing. In her spare time, she continues to speak at conferences across the globe and contribute weekly to her local newspaper.

ASHLEY M. JONES is Alabama State Poet Laureate (2022-2026). She received an MFA in Poetry from Florida International University (FIU), where she was a John S. and James L. Knight Foundation Fellow. Among many accomplishments, she was a finalist in the 2015 Hub City Press New Southern Voices Contest, the Crab Orchard Series in Poetry First Book Award Contest, and the National Poetry Series. Her poems and essays appear or are forthcoming in many journals and anthologies including CNN and the Academy of American Poets.

DR. BILL KING is a husband, father, grandfather, ordained minister, humorist, storyteller, speaker, songwriter, singer, musician, published author, syndicated columnist, and cancer survivor. He has published nine books—ranging from Christian novels to animated children's books—as well as recorded five CDs. In 2020, his weekly column placed second at the Southern Christian Writer's Conference, and in 2021, it placed first.

C.R. FULTON travels the east coast in an RV with her husband, two kids, and two dogs, Atlantic and Ocean. She is also a Young Living Executive, so marring oils with murder mystery writing seemed natural. She is the author of The Light of Andrea, a Robin Hood style action adventure series, and a spiritual thriller due in the 2021. Acrylic painting fuels her writing creativity, homeschooling her children keeps her sharp, but Jesus is the center of it all.

CHRISTAL ANN RICE COOPER is a newspaper writer, feature stories writer, poet, fiction writer, photographer, and painter. She has been writing for newspapers for over 25 years and currently runs her own personal blog and non-profit website which acknowledges ALL voices, ALL individuals, ALL political views, ALL philosophies, ALL religions.

GAYLE YOUNG, who spent most of her adult life working in an office and raising children, decided in retirement to indulge her lifelong interest in writing. Her first book, Redbirds, Roses, and Ghosts, won the 2019 Foreward INDIES bronze award for nonfiction humor. Her second book, Dirty Pink, was published in 2020. One of her life's regrets was that she did not attend college, so she is now a sophomore at a community college.

Photo
Not
Available

GUS GUESS is a pseudonym for the incarcerated author of scores of newspaper columns, a half dozen magazine articles, several unpublished books, and an ever-growing compilation of short stories. It is currently illegal in some Southern states to earn a living while under a sentence of penal servitude. Writing has enabled him to endure over thirty years of continuous inprisonment.

JENNIFER HORNE served as the twelfth Poet Laureate of Alabama from 2017 to 2021. She's the author of three collections of poems and a collection of short stories, and she has edited four volumes of poetry, essays, and stories. Her latest work is a biography of the writer Sara Mayfield, forthcoming from the University of Alabama Press.

KAREN ALLEN'S passions can be summed up in three words (aside from God, family, and her dogs): music, missions, and writing. Retired from cancer research, she fills her days writing, lunching with friends, and playing the organ. Her Bible study *Confronting Cancer with Faith* has brought hope around the world and her personal blog highlights blessings from life, cancer, and sheep!

LAURA HUNTER was raised in Alabama hill country and now lives near Tuscaloosa. She has published sixteen award-winning fiction pieces and nine poems, in addition to the numerous articles published through different media outlets. In 2020, Hunter released a collection of fictional short stories entitled *Southern Voices* which focuses on Copeland's Crossing, Alabama. Hunter's first novel *Beloved Mother,* released April 2019, has won numerous national and international awards.

M. E. HUBBS is an eleven year US Army Infantry veteran. He then served for 29 years as a historian and archaeologist for the U.S. Army Space and Missile Defense Command at Redstone Arsenal, retiring in December 2019. He has written and published non-fiction historical subjects for many years, but has more recently expanded into historical fiction for young readers.

Alabama dirt lurks stubbornly under the fingernails of lifetime farmer **MIKE WAHL**. More time for writing came only after retiring from a 48-year career working as an aerospace engineer. With writing efforts concentrated primarily on poetry, his poems have appeared in numerous print and on-line venues in recent years. He released one book of poetry in 2020 and has two more forthcoming this year.

PETE BLACK hails from Monroeville, Alabama, home of literary icons Harper Lee, Truman Capote and Pulitzer Prize winning journalist Cynthia Tucker. He is a civil engineering graduate from the University of Alabama who is retired after a 35-year career in the pulp and paper industry. Black writes 700-word non-fiction short stories about ordinary people who have overcome obstacles to accomplish extraordinary things. His short stories have been published in the GreyThoughts Writer's Club and a 52-story compilation of his work releases early 2022.

PETER LAST was very nearly born in an elevator and has continued to be unconventional ever since. He began writing his first novel, *Guardians of Magessa*, at the age of eleven, and has since released two trilogies (one to be complete in 2022). After earning his degree in Civil Engineering and commission in the United States military, he is now serving in the U.S. Air Force, protecting the nation from its enemies, termites, and HVAC outages. In the little spare time he has, Peter writes a blog, draws, and dabbles in film directing.

Gary Benton, a.k.a. **W. R. BENTON,** is an award-winning, best-selling author and Vietnam Veteran. He is the author of two survival books, *Simple Survival, A Family Outdoors Guide* and *Impending Disasters*, as well as over 70 other titles. When he's not writing his latest story, Benton enjoys hunting, hiking, camping, fishing, and meandering in the woods as well as freelancing outdoor and wilderness articles to various magazines and websites.

An author and motivational speaker who adores the power of words both written and spoken, at the end of 1996 this former BellSouth employee left 18 years of service and stepped out on faith as she pursues her purpose and passion—writing and speaking. **VANESSA DAVIS GRIGGS** is the author of 18 novels and has won countless awards for her work. She has most recently facilitatied writing workshops for the Birmingham Public Library, done motivational speaking engagements, and been the keynote speaker for various events.

CPSIA information can be obtained
at www.ICGtesting.com
Printed in the USA
FSHW011723121121

9 781949 711899